Being Julia

A Forever Novella

Sandi Lynn

Sandi Lynn

Being Julia (A Forever Novella)
Copyright © 2013 Sandi Lynn

All rights reserved. No part of this publication may be reproduced, distributed, or transmitted in any form or by any means, including photocopying, recording, or other electronic or mechanical methods without the prior written permission of the publisher.

This is a work of fiction. Names, characters, places and incidents are the products of the author's imagination or are used factitiously. Any resemblance to actual events, locales, or persons, living or dead, is entirely coincidental.

Cover Design by Cover It Designs

Photo Image: ID #10459372
www.shutterstock.com

Editing by B.Z. Hercules

Being Julia

Table of Contents

For All Of The Black Family Fans...4
Chapter 1 5
Sixteen 5
Chapter 2 12
Chapter 3 22
Chapter 4 34
Chapter 5 43
Chapter 6 53
Chapter 7 65
Chapter 8 72
Chapter 9 91
Chapter 10 99
Chapter 11 110
Chapter 12 121
Chapter 13 135
Chapter 14 148
Chapter 15 159
Chapter 16 171
Lie Next To Me 178
About The Author 182

Sandi Lynn

For all of the Black Family fans....

"A father is always making his baby into a little woman. And when she is a woman, he turns her back again."
~ Enid Bagnold

"The first true love any girl has, is her father. No one will ever replace him as the love of her life."
~ Unknown

"Certain is it that there is no kind of affection so purely angelic as of a father to a daughter. In love to our wives there is desire; to our sons, ambition; but to our daughters there is something which there are no words to express."
~Joseph Addison

Chapter 1

Sixteen

"Julia, it's time for dinner," my dad yelled up the stairs.

"I'll be right down, Dad," I said as I closed my laptop.

I walked downstairs and sat down just as Mom was putting the plate of breaded chicken on the table. Collin sat down shortly after I did and took a sip of his milk, which was in front of him. My mom finally sat down and smiled, letting us know that it was okay to begin eating.

"Have you talked to Hailey?" she asked as she looked at me.

"I talked to her yesterday. Why?"

"Peyton said she's been a little down lately and she thought maybe she mentioned something to you."

I cocked my head and gave her that "I'm sorry, but if I knew, I wouldn't tell you" look. "No, she hasn't said anything to me," I said.

Once she was convinced that I knew nothing, she darted her eyes to Collin. "What about you?"

"Uh…no. Why would she tell me anything?" he said as he tore into his chicken.

"I'll talk to her tomorrow, Mom." I smiled.

"Thank you, Julia."

My ears drowned out the voices of the conversations my family was having because my mind wouldn't stop thinking about Brody Sullivan and his hot, muscular body. There was nothing I wanted more than his strong arms wrapped around me.

"Hello, Earth to Julia," my dad said.

I snapped out of my fantasy world and looked at him. "What, Dad?"

"Where were you?"

There was no way I could tell him that I was dreaming about Brody. He was so protective. I was the only sixteen-year-old on the face of the planet that had never been on a date with a boy. But all that was going to change very soon.

"I'm right here, Dad." I replied with a sarcastic grin.

"I know you're right here, Julia. You're physically here, but your mind was somewhere else."

"No, it wasn't," I said as I shook my head.

My mom put her hand on my dad's, and he sighed. I got up from the table and put my plate in the sink. As I headed upstairs, Collin came up behind me.

"Hey, sis," he said.

"Yeah," I said as he stepped into my room and shut the door.

"I heard Brody talking about you today in school."

"Shut up! What was he saying?" I asked.

Collin sat on my bed and looked down at the floor. He was a really sweet kid, and even though I was older, he made it his business to look out for me.

"Well, what did he say?" I asked in anticipation.

"He said that he thinks you're hot and he wants to take you out," Collin replied as he looked up at me with the same eyes my father had.

I squealed as I jumped on the bed in excitement. Tingling sensations were shooting through my body as the thought of dating Brody Sullivan invaded my mind.

"Julia, he's bad news and I don't think you should go out with him. He's slept with almost every girl at Constantine Prep. He's a user, and I don't want you to get your hopes up. Plus, Dad will kill you!"

"I know how many girls he's slept with and it doesn't matter. I've had my eyes set on him for over three months. Dad isn't going to find out, is he, Collin?" I asked as I gave him a stern look.

He got up from the bed and shook his head. "No, he won't find out from me," he said as he walked out of my room.

I picked up my phone, sat down on my bed, and called my best friend, London.

"Hey, Julia, what's up?" she answered.

"Guess what? Collin just told me that Brody Sullivan thinks I'm hot and he wants to take me out!" I screeched into the phone.

"Shut the hell up! Collin knows this for sure?"

"Yes, he overheard him talking in school today."

"You're so lucky, Julia! I would kill to get into that boy's pants," she said.

"Hands off, London."

"I know." She sighed.

London Fitzgerald and I had been best friends since she moved into our building six years ago. She practically lived at my house because her family was so dysfunctional. Her father was a big time lawyer and was a partner at one of the biggest law firms in New York called Melbourne, Fitzgerald, and Holloway. Her mother was an alcoholic who usually started her day off at eight a.m. with a glass of orange juice and vodka. Her father had had multiple affairs, and they fought non-stop. She loved to spend time at my house because of the relationship my mother and father had. Sometimes, it was really embarrassing because they couldn't keep their hands off each other and they'd have make-out sessions in the kitchen. London wished her family were like mine. She said that every time she walked into the penthouse, she could feel the love. Mom and Dad spoiled her as if she were their own daughter. They felt sorry for her because of her crappy home life. I felt bad for her too, and I was sure it was the reason for her being so promiscuous. She only wanted to be loved.

I sat down at my desk and opened my laptop. I had so much homework to do and it was all due tomorrow; there was no mercy at Constantine Prep School for Girls. I was working on my calculus when a friend request on Skype came through. I clicked on it and gasped when I saw that it was from Brody Sullivan. My heart started racing and it felt like someone had turned up the heat in my body. I pointed the cursor to "add to contacts" and clicked. As I not so patiently waited to see what he'd do next, I sent a text message to London.

"OMG! Brody just friend requested me on Skype!"

A few seconds later, she replied, *"No way! He's so into you! I can't wait until school tomorrow!"*

I stared at my screen, waiting, and tapping my fingers on my desk. Suddenly, a message from him popped up.

"Hey, Julia, thanks for accepting. I was wondering if I could have your phone number."

My heart was still pounding as the butterflies in my stomach were fluttering around like they were high. I placed my hands on the keyboard and typed in my phone number. A few seconds later, my phone beeped.

"Thanks for your number. I was wondering if you wanted to do something tomorrow after school."

Excitement overtook my mind, and I felt like I was going to die, but I needed to remain calm and not show too much excitement, so I waited five minutes before I sent my reply.

"Hey, no problem. I would like to hang out after school."

"Awesome. I'll meet you outside of Constantine's tomorrow. Then we can decide what to do."

"Okay. I'll see you tomorrow," I replied with a grin across my face.

What could I say about Brody Sullivan? He was an eighteen-year-old godly creature who attended St. Matthews Prep School for Boys, which sat next to Constantine's. His short, light brown hair with messy bangs swept to the side and bright blue eyes, which drew you into him, were just a couple of things that made him incredibly sexy. His flat, washboard stomach and muscular arms were the result of his working out at the gym every day. His father was a Chief Risk Officer on Wall Street, and his mother was a jewelry designer who owned her own high-end jewelry line. He had a "playboy" reputation, but as I saw it, he just hadn't found the right girl yet. But, I was about to change all that and him.

Chapter 2

As I searched my closet for something to wear, there was a knock on the door.

"Come in. Morning, Mom." I smiled as she walked into my room.

"I was just coming to wake you up. But I see you're already up and showered."

"Yeah, I just didn't want to run late today," I said as I took out my cream-colored baby doll dress from the closet.

She gave me a weird look as she said, "Okay," and walked out the door.

I put on my dress, my high-heeled brown ankle boots, curled my blonde hair, put on a little more makeup than usual, and went downstairs for breakfast. When I entered the kitchen, my dad, who was sitting at the table, looked up from his phone.

"You're early today," he said.

"Morning, Daddy," I said as I grabbed a glass of orange juice from the counter and walked over and kissed him on the cheek.

"Morning, Princess. Don't you think that dress is a little too short to be wearing?" he asked.

I rolled my eyes and sighed. "Mom!" I said.

"Connor, her dress is fine. It's what all the girls wear, plus, if it was too short, she wouldn't be allowed to wear it to school."

He looked at me and smiled. "I still think it's too short."

"Of course you do, Dad. You think everything is too short. You're just going to have to get used to the fact that I'm sixteen now, and I can wear what I want." I winked as I grabbed a piece of toast and walked out of the kitchen.

Before I grabbed my school bag, I walked back into the kitchen and over to my dad. I wrapped my arms around his neck and kissed him on the cheek.

"What was that for?" He smiled.

I put on my princess face and I replied, "I'm sorry if I had an attitude, Daddy. Can I please have the credit card so London and I can go shopping after school? I promise to buy longer dresses and skirts." I smiled.

He looked at me as he reached in his pocket, pulled out his wallet, and handed me his credit card. "No short dresses," he said.

"Thank you, Daddy. I love you."

"I love you too, baby." He smiled.

Being Julia

As I started to walk out of the kitchen, I stopped and turned around. "Since I'm sixteen, don't you think it would be best if I had my own credit card so I don't have to keep asking you?"

He looked at me and cocked his head, but didn't say anything. I could tell he was thinking about it. I kissed my mom goodbye as she shook her head at me, and I took the elevator to the garage. Collin was already in the limo.

"It's about time, Julia!" he said.

"Sorry, but I had to ask Dad for the credit card."

Denny looked at me through the rearview mirror and smiled. "Good morning, Miss Julia."

"Good morning, Uncle Denny." I smiled back. "I won't need a ride home today. London and I are going shopping after school."

****

The day couldn't have gone by any slower that it already was. The only thing that was on my mind was seeing Brody after school. Nothing of the day mattered but him. I told London that I had told my parents we were going shopping after school, and she'd told her mom the same thing because she was meeting up with Rob at Starbucks. He was the twenty-three-year-old that she'd been seeing for a couple of weeks. *That* was another story.

The last bell of the day finally rang and, instantly, the butterflies woke up. I grabbed London's arm and we headed out the doors and down the steps of Constantine's. As I checked my phone to see if I had received a text message from Brody, he came up behind me.

"Hey, Julia. You look great." He smiled.

I bit down on my bottom lip and smiled back at him. He hooked his arm around me, claiming me as his, and we walked down the busy streets of New York. I could see Collin in the distance, shaking his head at me.

"So what do you want to do?" Brody asked.

He was so sweet, asking me what I wanted to do, and I couldn't believe he had his arm around me. "It doesn't matter. Do you want to go see a movie?"

"Alone with you in a dark movie theater? Sounds good to me." He winked.

We walked a couple of blocks over to the movie theater, where he bought my ticket, popcorn, and soda. We took our seats and, while we waited for the movie to begin, Brody took a piece of popcorn and put it in my mouth.

"You're really hot." He smiled.

I could feel myself blush as I looked at him and smiled. "I think you're really hot too."

He took another piece of popcorn from the bag and traced my lips with his finger before putting the popcorn in my mouth. I smiled as I took it and he leaned closer and softly brushed his lips against mine.

"Your lips are so soft." He moaned as his mouth pushed firmly into mine.

The lights dimmed and the movie started playing. He broke our kiss, but not before slipping his tongue in my mouth. It was the most amazing kiss I'd ever had. Not that I'd had that many, but his was breathtaking. He left me speechless as he smiled at me, and then turned to watch the movie. When the movie was over, he took my hand and led me out of the theater. His limo was waiting for us at the curb. As I slid in, he sat down next to me and put up the tinted privacy window.

"That was a great movie, wasn't it?" I asked.

"Yeah, real good," he said as he leaned closer to me, cupped my chin in his hand, and kissed me.

As our tongues collided with each other and his scent aroused my senses, he took his hand and stuck it down the front of my dress, cupping my breast in his hand. I was startled because no one had ever done that to me.

"It's okay, babe. I just want to feel your tits," he said between kisses.

Once he removed his hand, he unbuttoned his jeans, took my hand, and placed it down his pants, making me feel his erection. "Feel how excited you get me, Julia."

I moved my hand up and down as a moan came from inside his chest. I couldn't believe I was doing this, but I didn't want to disappoint him. He put his hand up my dress and began moving it up my thigh. He reached my panties and I stopped.

"No, Brody," I said as I broke our kiss.

He looked at me and smiled. "I'm sorry. It's just that you got me so excited that I wanted to feel if you were too."

The limo pulled up in front of my building. Before getting out of the limo, I looked around to make sure there was nobody I knew in sight.

"I'll talk to you later, babe." He smiled as he let go of my hand.

"Yeah, later," I said as my head was stuck way up in the clouds.

The moment I stepped off the elevator, my mom walked over to me. "Hi, honey. Where are your bags?" she asked.

"What bags?"

"Shopping bags. Didn't you buy anything?"

"Oh," I said, forgetting that I told her that London and I were going shopping. "No, I really didn't see anything I liked."

"Julia, you always find things you like," she said.

Oh my God, what was with the interrogation? I thought to myself. "I know, right? I did see a couple of dresses I liked, but they were out of my size," I said as I started to walk up to my bedroom.

"Don't forget; we're going out to dinner tonight. Just the four of us."

"I didn't forget, Mom," I yelled from the top of the stairs.

As I stepped into my room, I went to shut the door and Collin stopped it.

"How was your afternoon with the playboy?"

I rolled my eyes as I threw my purse on the bed. "We had a great time. We went to the movies and now I'm home."

"Listen, Julia. I don't want you to get your hopes up with him. He's a player and you deserve better than that," Collin said.

"I'm a big girl, little brother. I can take care of myself. Now, if you'll excuse me, I'm going to freshen up before we go to dinner."

Collin left my room, and I walked into the bathroom. As I stared at myself in the mirror, I ran my finger along my lips, remembering the amazing kisses Brody and I had shared. I snapped back to reality when I heard my phone chime. I looked down and saw there was a text message from Brody.

"Hey, babe. I can't stop thinking about you. I miss you already."

A huge smile spread across my face as I instantly replied.

"Hi, I was just remembering our kiss. I miss you too."

Collin knocked on my door and told me we were leaving for dinner. I put on my boots and walked downstairs as my dad was putting on his coat.

"Hi, Daddy." I smiled as I gave him a kiss on the cheek.

"Hi, Princess. How was your day?" he asked as he hugged me.

"It was good."

"How much did you spend?"

"You're going to be so proud of me. I didn't spend a dime." I smiled.

He looked at me and cocked his head in confusion. "Seriously, Julia. How much did you spend?"

"Seriously, Dad, I spent nothing. They didn't have my size in the couple of things I saw," I replied with a pout.

"Aw, I'm sorry. Maybe next time," he said as he held his hand out for his card.

My mom and Collin emerged from the kitchen and asked us if we were ready to go. We climbed into the Range Rover and headed to the restaurant. It was very important to my mom that we ate dinner as a family at least three nights a week. So my dad made sure that at least one night a week, we ate out at a restaurant and, no matter where we were, we had to meet there. While we were sitting and waiting for our food, my dad reached in his pocket and handed me what looked like a credit card.

Being Julia

"I got this for you." He smiled.

I reached across the table and took it from him. I examined it; it had my name on it.

"Daddy, thank you so much!"

"You're welcome, sweetheart. I ordered it last week and when you said something about your own credit card this morning, I wanted to tell you, but I wanted to surprise you with it."

I got out of my seat, walked over to his side, and hugged him tight. "I love you, Dad."

"I love you, too, baby. You better be careful with it and don't overspend. I'm trusting you enough to give you that responsibility."

"Don't worry. I'll be careful," I said as I sat back down.

My mom looked at me and smiled as she put her arm around him and rested her head on his shoulder. He turned and kissed her head. As embarrassing as it was to have my parents being all touchy feely in public, it was nice to see how in love they were. I started to think about Brody, so I took out my phone and sent him a text message.

"Hi, I'm at dinner with my parents, and I was thinking about you."

"Hi. Good thoughts, I hope."

"Only the best."

He replied back with a smiley face and I was in Heaven.

Chapter 3

Over the next few days, Brody and I continued to see each other after school, and every day we went a little further. He wasn't pressuring me to have sex, but he said that he couldn't wait and, the more he thought about it, the more he couldn't wait. Brody asked me out on a real date, and I was so excited. He told me he'd pick me up, and that meant one thing; he'd have to meet Connor and Ellery. The thought of him meeting my parents made me extremely nervous. I wasn't sure how my dad was going to react since I wasn't allowed to date yet. If he only knew. I walked into the living where my parents were snuggled on the couch.

"Hey, Mom and Dad." I smiled. "I need to discuss something with you."

My mom sat up and looked at me. "Okay, honey, what is it?"

I took in a deep breath as nervousness flowed throughout my body.

"Do you need to sit down?" my dad asked.

"Julia, whatever it is, just say it," my mom said.

I sat down in the chair that sat across from them. "There's someone I would like you to meet because we're going out tomorrow." *There, I said it*, I thought as I let out a breath.

"What's his name?" my mom asked with a small smile.

"It better not be a 'him,'" my dad immediately said.

He was starting already and not giving me a chance. Instantly, my defenses went up.

"His name is Brody," I answered as I looked at my mom. "He goes to St. Matthews, and he's eighteen."

As I kept my eyes focused on my mom, I could feel my dad's glare burning into my skin.

"No," he said.

"Connor," my mom said as she grabbed his hand.

"No, Ellery. She's not going out on a date."

I loved my dad, but sometimes he really sucked, and he needed to stop being so protective.

"Dad, why?" I whined.

"Because, Julia. You don't need that complication in your life right now. You have your paintings and school to focus on. Not some boy whose only concern is getting in your pants."

"DAD! Brody isn't like that! He's really sweet and caring, and he likes me a lot. Mom, please do something."

"Connor, she's sixteen. Come on. You remember what it was like when you were sixteen."

"Exactly, and that's why she's not allowed to date. I only had one thing on my mind at that age," he said. "Sorry, Princess, but the answer is no."

I stood there and shook my head him. "Would it make you feel better if I told you I was a lesbian?" I shouted.

As he sat there, he slowly shook his head and glared at me with angry eyes. "You may go to your room now, Julia."

When I started to walk away, I stopped, turned around, and looked at him with tears in my eyes. "For the record, I know what a man-whore you used to be until you met Mom, so you have no right!"

"Julia!" my mom exclaimed.

I stomped up the stairs in a huff and slammed my bedroom door as hard as I could. I threw myself on my bed as I lay there face down and sobbed into my pillow. My phone beeped with a text message from Collin.

"Are you okay, sis?"

"No. I hate him," I replied back.

There was a soft knock on the door, and my mom walked in. She sat down on the bed next to me and started to rub my back.

"Julia, please don't cry."

"I don't want to talk to you, Mom. Please get out," I said in between sobs.

"You can go out with him, Julia. Just make sure he comes to the door when he picks you up so we can meet him first."

I sniffed and turned my head. "Really? You're going to let me go out with him?"

She took a tissue from my nightstand and handed it to me. "Yes, you may go out with him."

"But what about Dad?"

She pursed her lips as she gave me a small smile. "I've handled your dad. So don't worry. But you need to understand that he's only trying to protect you and, believe me, I know he goes overboard sometimes. But, he does it out of love, Julia."

"Thanks, Mom," I said as I hugged her tightly.

"Dry your tears and go to bed." She smiled as she walked to the door. She stopped and turned around. "I love you, Julia. Don't ever doubt that."

"I love you too, Mom." I smiled back.

****

The next morning, I got dressed and went downstairs for breakfast. My dad was sitting at the table, drinking his coffee. I could feel him staring at me.

"Good morning, Julia."

"Morning," I said in a short tone.

I grabbed a bowl, poured some cereal and milk in it, and then took it over to the table. I wouldn't look at him because I was still mad at him, and I felt bad for what I'd said.

"This boy you're interested in; is his name Brody Sullivan?" he asked.

I looked up from my cereal bowl. "Yes."

"He comes from a good and successful family. He'll be picking you up tonight?"

"Yes," I answered softly.

"Well, then, I guess I'll be meeting him tonight before he takes you out on a—"

"*Date*, Connor. He'll be picking her up and taking her on a *date*," my mom said as she walked into the kitchen.

He looked at her and pursed his lips. "I know that, Ellery. Why do you have to keep emphasizing that word?"

I couldn't help but laugh as I got up from the table and starting walking out of the kitchen.

"Julia?" my dad said after he cleared his throat.

I turned around and he had his finger on his cheek. I smiled as I walked over to him and gave him a kiss goodbye.

****

"How nervous are you that Brody is meeting your parents?" London asked as she lay across my bed.

"Very nervous. I'm not worried about Ellery. It's my dad I'm worried about. God knows what kind of interrogation he'll put Brody through."

"So, are you going to have sex tonight?" she asked.

I peeked my head out of my walk-in closet and smiled. "I don't know; we'll see. Do you have any tips for me?"

"No, but it does hurt the first time, so prepare yourself. Remember the first time I did it? I came to you crying afterwards because it was awful."

"I remember. But I also remember that it was John's first time too and you said he didn't know what he was doing. I don't have to worry about that with Brody. He has plenty of experience."

"Just make sure you use protection, Julia," she said.

"Don't worry. I'm not stupid."

I slipped on my black leggings, a long beaded tank top, and my short black jacket. I needed to make sure my ass was covered or my dad wouldn't let me out of the penthouse. I curled my long blonde hair and looked at the time. Brody was going to be here any minute.

"Don't forget your tall black boots." London smiled as she handed them to me.

We walked downstairs to the living room and my mom was sitting on the couch, looking through an art magazine.

"You look amazing, sweetheart." She smiled.

"Thanks, Mom. Where's Dad?"

"He's in his office. Good luck. Let me know if he gets out of hand."

London sat down next to my mom and looked at the art magazine with her, while I stepped into my dad's office. He looked up at me and just stared.

"Well?" I asked as I turned around in circle.

"You look exactly like your mom." He smiled. "You look beautiful, Princess."

"Thanks, Daddy."

My mom called my name and told me that Brody had arrived. I took in a deep breath as my dad followed me out of his office.

"You be nice," I said.

"I'm always nice, Julia."

We reached the living room, where Brody was talking to my mom and London. I smiled at him and said hi, and then proceeded to introduce him to Connor Black.

"Brody, this is my dad. Dad, this is Brody Sullivan."

The two of them shook hands. I wanted to get the hell out of there as fast as I could before my dad had a chance to ask any questions. My phone beeped, and when I looked at it, there was a text message from London.

"Look at the way your dad's staring him down."

I shot London a look from across the room and then took Brody's hand and led him to the elevator.

"We better get going." I smiled.

"Have my daughter home by midnight, Mr. Sullivan," my dad yelled from across the room.

"Don't worry, Mr. Black, I'll have her home on time. She'll be safe with me."

I turned and looked at my dad as he watched us step onto the elevator.

"Have fun, you two." My mom waved.

Being Julia

****

Connor

As soon as the elevator door shut, I walked over to the bar and poured myself a scotch. Ellery stood on the other side of the room, staring at me.

"What?" I asked.

"He seems like a really nice boy. He was polite, proper, and very well dressed."

"Those are the ones you have to watch out for," I said as I held up my glass.

The fact was that I wasn't ready to release my little girl out into the dating world. Ellery convinced me that sixteen was the appropriate age to start dating. She also threatened me. I knew Julia wasn't perfect, but she was still my princess and she always would be. It was a miracle that she was even conceived. The odds were against her, between the reversal of my vasectomy and Ellery's treatments.

"Look at you. You can't stand this, can you?" Ellery asked as put her arms around me.

"No, I can't. I hate the fact that my baby girl is out with some random guy doing God knows what."

"I've educated her, Connor. She's a smart girl and she'll make the right choices."

"I hope so, Elle," I said as I kissed her lips.

"You need a distraction. I'm going to call Peyton and see if they want to come over for pizza."

"Sounds good, sweetheart." I smiled as I poured another Scotch.

Being Julia

****

Ellery

I walked into the kitchen, took my phone from the counter, and dialed Peyton.

"Hello, friend," she answered.

"Hi, Pey. I wanted to know if you, Henry, and Hailey would like to come over for pizza? Julia went out on her first date and Connor can't relax. He's going crazy, and I think Henry would be a good distraction for him."

"Sure, Elle. We can do that. I was just about to start dinner. Now I don't have to cook. Henry should be home in a few minutes, so we'll be over within the hour."

"Thanks, Peyton."

"Any time, Elle."

I walked into the living room. Connor was sitting on the couch with Collin, looking at his laptop. "Henry, Peyton, and Hailey will be here within the hour. I already ordered the pizzas and salads."

"Hailey's coming over?" Collin asked.

"Yes," I replied.

He got up from the couch and went upstairs. "Where are you going?" I asked.

"I forgot something in my room," he said.

Before I sat down, I took the laptop from Connor and set it on the table. He held out his arms and I sat down on his lap. I smiled at him as I ran my fingers through his hair.

"Don't worry about Julia. She'll be fine."

"How the hell can you be so calm?" he asked.

"Because it's a date, Connor. A date of dinner, talking, and laughter."

"I don't know, Elle. I don't trust him."

Collin ran down the stairs and grabbed his laptop. The scent of Hollister cologne followed him.

"Did you just go upstairs and put on cologne?" I asked.

"Umm…no, it's from earlier."

"That's funny. I didn't smell anything on you earlier." I smirked.

"Mom, please. Why are you making a big deal about it?"

"Yeah, Mom. What's the big deal?" Connor smiled at me.

"This wouldn't have anything to do with Hailey coming over, would it?"

"Mom! Stop!" Collin exclaimed as he headed up the stairs.

Connor and I looked at each other. "That's my boy," he said.

Chapter 4

Brody took me to Per Se, where we ate the finest cuisines. For someone his age, he sure knew how to impress. We were sitting across from each other and he stared at me. Those blue eyes burned into me and put me under a spell.

"Has anyone ever told you how beautiful you are?" he asked.

I smiled as I blushed. "I bet you say that to all the girls."

"Actually, I don't. I might tell them they're hot. But you, you're better than hot. You're the most beautiful girl in the world."

I placed my hand on the table and he took it in his. We talked about our family and school. He told me that he planned to go to Harvard Law and become one of the best attorneys in the world. After we ate our amazing meal, we climbed into the back of his limo and made out. I wanted nothing more than his lips all over me. As things were really heating up and getting intense, he broke our kiss and looked at me.

"I need to have sex with you, Julia, but not here in the back of my limo. How about tomorrow? Do you think you're ready yet?"

I was breathless as I answered, "Yes, let's do it tomorrow. Where?" I asked.

"I would say at my house, but my mom is hosting some jewelry party, so that's out of the question. How about your house?"

"My house would be perfect." I smiled. "My mom and dad are flying to Chicago for the day and my brother is going out with my grandfather, so we'll have the house to ourselves all day." I smiled.

"Perfect," he said as he nipped at my bottom lip and his hand traveled up my shirt.

Brody dropped me off five minutes before my curfew. He said that my dad would be pleased about that. I stepped off the elevator, and I felt like I was on Cloud Nine. I heard the TV in the living room, so I walked in there to see my mom and dad lying together on the couch and my mom sleeping.

"Hi, Dad," I whispered.

"How was your date?" he whispered back.

"It was nice, thank you."

"Why don't you go up to bed now and we can talk about it in the morning?" he said.

"Goodnight." I smiled as I leaned over and kissed him on the cheek.

I walked up to my room and immediately sent a text message to London. I told her about my night and how, come tomorrow, I'd no longer be a virgin. She was excited, but said she had to go, she was with Rob, the older guy. As I changed into my pajamas, I stared at myself in the mirror thinking about how Brody said I was the most beautiful girl in the world. He was so sweet and kind that I didn't believe any of the rumors about him. They didn't matter anyway. I was his girl and his only. At least after tomorrow, I would be.

****

I couldn't sleep the whole night, thanks to Brody Sullivan. Every time I closed my eyes, he was all I saw and felt. I swore I could still feel his lips against mine. I got up and headed down the hallway. I heard my mom and dad talking in their bedroom so I decided to knock on the door.

"Mom, Dad, can I come in?"

"Sure, sweetheart," my mom said as she opened the door. She took my hand and, with a big smile, she led me over to her bed and made me sit down. "How was your date? I want to hear all about it."

"It was amazing, Mom. He took me to Per Se and we ate the most amazing food and had the most amazing conversation." I smiled.

"The boy sure doesn't spare any expense, does he?" my dad said as he came from the bathroom.

"Did you with Mom?" I asked him.

"That's different, Julia. We weren't sixteen and eighteen years old. We were adults."

"Really? So you sending over a bunch of designer dresses, shoes, and jewelry for her to pick from for your charity event when you only had known her, what? Two days? Was acceptable?"

He looked at me, cocked his head, and then looked at my mom. He shook his head and didn't say a word as he grabbed his wallet off the dresser and put it in his pocket. He started to walk out of the bedroom, but he stopped and turned around.

"For the record, I was already in love with her." He winked at my mom.

"You know, Mom, you never told me how you and Daddy met."

She took my hand and smiled. "We'll talk about another time. It's quite a story. So, what are your plans today while we're in Chicago?"

"London is coming over and we're just going to look through fashion magazines and watch movies."

I hated lying to her; it killed me. She patted my hand and smiled. I turned her wrist over and lightly ran my finger over her tattoo. "I love this tattoo. Is there a story behind it other than how much you love Daddy?"

Her lips formed a small smile as she got up from the bed. "When you're older, we can talk about that." She winked.

As we walked downstairs, I hugged my dad goodbye.

"Bye, Dad. Have a safe flight."

"Bye, Princess. Make sure you don't go anywhere and stay safe. If you need something, call your Uncle Mason or Uncle Denny," he said as he kissed me on the head.

"I'm sixteen, Dad. How many times do I need to remind you of that? I'm surprised you're not having someone babysit me."

He looked at my mom right after I said that. "Mom!" I exclaimed.

"Julia, don't worry. I put the idea right out of his head." She smiled at me, kissed me goodbye, and then stepped onto the elevator.

I waited about thirty minutes to make sure they were gone and out of sight before sending a text to Brody.

"Hi, my parents left, so it's safe for you to come over."

"Hi, I'll be over in five!"

I ran up to my room and looked at myself in the full-length mirror. I ran my hands through my hair and brought it over my shoulders. As I rummaged through my drawer for my lace thong, I heard the doorbell ring. I hurried and pulled out my black one, slipped it on, flew down the stairs, and opened the door. Brody stood there, smiling and checking me out from head to toe.

"Look at you, babe, all hot and sexy."

I grabbed his hand, led him into the penthouse, and kissed him on the lips.

"I've missed you." I smiled.

"Yeah, me too, babe."

I led him to the living room and we sat on the couch. He leaned me back and starting running his lips across my neck as his hand traveled up my shirt. I grabbed his hand and pushed him back.

"Let's wait a little bit. We don't have to do it right away," I said.

"Yes, we do, Julia. I've been waiting for this for moment. I've wanted this since I first laid eyes on you. You're so hot; I can only imagine what it feels like to be inside you. You're going to be so tight and amazing, and I'm going to show you what it's all about. Let me introduce you to the world of sex and how amazing it is, Julia. Please. We're going to be so good together." He smiled.

Every time he smiled, it melted my heart. He had me under his spell. I got up from the couch, took his hand, and led him upstairs to my bedroom. As we stood next to the bed, Brody lifted off my shirt and threw it on the floor. He stared into my eyes as his fingers deftly unhooked my bra.

"Look at how perfect your tits are. I knew they'd be," he said as he took them in his mouth.

Before pushing me down onto the bed, he slid off my skirt and gripped my ass firmly with his hands. "So perfect. So perfect," he whispered between kisses.

Nerves had taken over me, and I kept telling myself that this would be okay. He knew what he was doing, and he'd make me comfortable. But comfortable wasn't what I was feeling. He took my hand and guided it down the front of his pants. I felt so stupid because I didn't know what I was doing. He told me just to relax and he would help me. He took down my thong and plunged a finger inside me. I flinched because it hurt.

"Relax, babe," he said.

As his finger was inside me, I took down his pants and underwear, taking note of the "not as big as I thought" package below. He stopped what he was doing and told me to pull back the covers and lie down as he removed a condom from his pants pocket. I did as he asked and watched him as he tore open the packet and slid on the piece of rubber, which was going to keep me from getting pregnant, over his dick. I took in a deep breath as he climbed on top of me and pulled the covers over us. He pushed back my hair as he hovered over me and smiled. His smile was so warm and caring that I was becoming less nervous. He tried to insert himself into me and I let out a whimper. It hurt like hell and he barely did anything.

"You're too dry, babe. Let me get you wet," he said as he went down on me. "There. Now you should be ready."

The fact was that I wasn't, but I wasn't about to let Brody know that. He pushed himself into me, and it was weird. There was a slight pain, but nothing like I had expected. Before I knew it, he was fully inside me and I was having sex. I was no longer a virgin. He moved in and out of me slowly, asking me if I was okay with each thrust. He smashed his mouth into mine as light moans came from the back of his throat. His last thrust was hard as he yelled my name while he came inside me. He looked at me and kissed my lips softly.

"Did you come, Julia?" he asked.

I didn't know what to say because I wasn't sure if I did or not. I didn't want to hurt his feelings, so I told him yes.

He climbed off of me, took off the condom, and flushed it down the toilet. He walked back into the room and climbed back into bed. After he wrapped his arms around me, he asked me a question.

"How was it? Did you enjoy it?"

"Yeah, it was good," I said with hesitation.

Being Julia

His hand started kneading my breast as I looked up at him, and he kissed me. He wanted to have sex again, but I didn't want to. As he rolled me on my back, his mouth forcefully pushed against mine, forcing my lips to part so his tongue could explore my mouth again. He hovered over me and I could feel his erection in between my legs. I kissed him back with pleasure, but I was too sore to have sex again. As I was about to break our kiss and tell him, my door opened. Brody jumped up as he saw my dad standing in the doorway. My heart started racing, and I felt like I was going to pass out.

Chapter 5

"What the FUCK is going on?!" my dad screamed.

Suddenly, my mom came up behind him and looked at me, shaking her head.

"Get the fuck out of my house," my dad yelled as he grabbed Brody's clothes and threw them at him.

My mom grabbed my dad and made him go downstairs. "Julia, get dressed right now," she yelled. "Brody, you need to leave this second before I throw you out, dressed or not."

Brody looked at me as he walked out of my bedroom. "I'll call you later," he said as he shut the door.

I was shaking so badly, I couldn't stand up. Every time I did, I'd fall back down on the bed. I felt sick, and I wanted to throw up. My parents caught me having sex. *What the hell am I going to do? I can't face them, especially my dad. He's going to murder me and, as of right now, my life, as I know it, is over.* I struggled to put on my skirt and my shirt as I heard my dad screaming my name from downstairs. I ran to the bathroom to throw up. When I was finished, I walked downstairs and into the living room where my parents were. My dad was at the bar, kicking back a glass of scotch, while my mom was sitting on the couch with her face buried in her hands. My dad slammed his glass down on the bar and pointed his finger at me.

"You, you are in serious trouble, young lady. What the hell were you thinking?" he yelled.

"Connor, calm down. Julia, come sit next to me," my mom said.

"Don't tell me to calm down, Ellery. What the hell is the matter with you? We walk in our sixteen-year-old daughter having sex and you tell me to calm down? If you think this is okay, then we have a serious problem."

I could see my mom's eyes burning into my dad as she stared at him. I'd never seen him so angry before, and he scared me. He stared at me and shook his head.

"I am so disappointed and so disgusted that I can't even look at you."

The tears that I tried to hold back started streaming down my face as the person who I loved most in the world looked at me with shame.

"I'm sorry, Daddy," I cried.

"Sorry? You're sorry? Sorry for what, Julia? That you got caught?"

I started to sob as my mom put her arm around me and pulled me into her.

He walked over and stood over me. "You're grounded for the rest of your life. Denny will drive you and pick you up from school every day. You will not see any of your friends, including London, and I'm shutting off your phone and taking your computer away. Consider yourself a prisoner in this house."

"But, Daddy," I sobbed as I looked at him.

"NO BUTS! You're grounded!" he screamed.

I got up from the couch and stood in front of him. My breathing was rapid and a fire was burning fiercely inside me. "I hate you," I said.

My dad looked away from me as I saw the tears in his eyes. I turned and looked at my mom, who was sitting there, crying.

"Thanks for your support, Mom. It's something I'll never forget," I said as I ran upstairs to my room and slammed the door shut.

I threw myself on my bed and sobbed. Moments later, my dad came into my room and took my laptop from my desk.

"Give me your phone, Julia," he demanded.

I took it from the bed and threw it against the wall as hard as I could. Needless to say, it broke. He walked out of my room and, before shutting the door, he said, "Don't come out of here for the rest of the day."

I got up from my bed and slammed my fists against the door. I paced back and forth across the floor before I fell to my knees and continued to sob. After a while, I heard the door open and then softly close.

"Julia, are you okay?" Collin asked.

"I hate them both," I sobbed.

He put his arm around me and helped me off the floor. "You don't mean that. You're just upset right now."

"I do mean it, Collin. You should have seen him and the look in his eyes. They were filled with rage and disgust. I thought he was going to kill me."

"It's almost dinner time; do you want me to bring you something up?" he asked.

"No, I'm not hungry, but thanks," I said as I hugged him.

"I'm really sorry this happened, Julia."

"I know you are, baby brother. I think I'm going to take a shower. Could you please do me a favor and text London and tell her what happened?"

"Sure, I'll do that right now." He smiled.

I got up from the bed and decided to take a bath instead. I started the water and poured a capful of bubbles under the stream. I climbed in and lay back, letting the hot water soothe my body. I closed my eyes as the tears fell down my face once again. I was thinking about everything that happened when I heard the bathroom door open, and I heard my mom whisper my name.

"Get out. I don't want to talk to you," I cried.

"I'm sorry, but I'm not leaving. I'm your mom, and you're going to talk to me whether you want to or not," she said as she sat down on the floor next to the tub.

"Please just go away and leave me alone," I whispered.

My mom took my hand, which was sitting on the tub, turned it over, and softly rubbed my wrist. "The tattoos I have on each of my wrists are covering up the scars of my attempted suicide when I was your age."

I opened my eyes and looked at her, horrified by what she just told me. "Mom."

"I guess it's time you knew about my past. You already know that my mom died when I was a little girl, and I've told you how hard it was on your grandfather. I was diagnosed with cancer on my sixteenth birthday."

My heart felt like it stopped beating when my mom said that. I had no idea that she'd been sick or that she had attempted suicide. "Mom," I said as I put my hand on her cheek.

She took my hand and pressed my palm against her lips as she smiled softly. "I couldn't let your grandfather go through that again, so I thought it was best that I spared him the pain. I figured it would be easier for him to get over my death than to have to see me so sick and then die."

Being Julia

"How could you think that?" I asked as tears swelled in my eyes.

"Because I was sixteen years old. He became an alcoholic because of what happened to my mother. Anyway, he came home one night and found me and called an ambulance. The doctors saved me, and I went through a year of chemo and went into remission."

The tears that were in my eyes fell quickly as I stared into my mother's eyes. They were full of sadness and despair as she told her heart-wrenching story. She handed me a towel and told me that if I stayed any longer in the bath, I'd turn into a prune. She walked out of the bathroom and told me she'd wait for me to get dressed. As I stepped out of the tub, I wrapped the towel around me and looked at myself in the mirror. I started to believe that there was more to my mom and her past I didn't know about. I put on my robe, walked into my bedroom, and sat down on the bed next to her. I grabbed her hand and turned it over, staring at the tattoo that said my father's name on her wrist.

"Your dad got kicked out of a club for being so drunk that he was causing a scene. I had already noticed him that night, and when I walked outside to get some fresh air, he was sitting up against the brick wall. I hailed a cab, helped him into it and took him home."

"Mom, that's dangerous. You just don't do stuff like that. Even I know better than that."

She smiled at me and kissed the side of my head. "You sound like your father. He got sick all over his clothes when I brought him here to the penthouse, and I couldn't let him sit in his own vomit all night, so I undressed him and made sure he was safe in his bed. When I went to check on him one last time before I left, he was on his back, so I rolled him on his side and sat next to him all night to make sure he didn't throw up again. That's how your grandfather died. He choked to death on his own vomit. I ended up falling asleep and, when I woke up, it was morning."

I lay down on my back and my mom lay next to me. "What did Dad say when he woke up and found you lying next to him?"

"I wanted to get out of the penthouse before he woke up, so I went down to the kitchen, made a pot of coffee, and made my famous hangover cocktail. I was going to leave a note with the drink when he came into the kitchen and scared the shit of me."

"What did he say to you?" I asked.

She looked over at me and smiled. "Your father had a list of rules and he thought that I had broken one of them."

"That's weird. What kind of rules did he have?"

"That's something I don't think your father would want me to talk about with you."

"I've heard stories, you know. Stories about him and all the women he dated when he was younger. Some of the stories aren't so nice."

My mom took my hand and interlaced our fingers. "All that stopped when he met me, and your father became the man he was destined to be. Listen, Julia, your dad loves you and this family more than anything in the whole world. He's acting out of anger right now and he'll eventually calm down. But we need to talk about what went on here today. I want nothing but an open and honest relationship with you and I thought that's what we had. To be honest with you, I'm very hurt that you felt you couldn't come to me and talk to me about having sex with this boy."

Tears started to fill my eyes again as I looked up at the ceiling. "I'm sorry. I couldn't talk to you because you would tell Dad or you'd lecture me and try to talk me out of it. I think I love him, Mom."

"Oh, Julia, love is so complicated. You may think you love him, but at sixteen, it's hard for you to understand what love is. You're going to have so many more boyfriends that you think you love, until that one special person who knocks the breath right out of you, looks at you."

"I bet you had a lot of boyfriends at my age."

"I dated a couple of guys, but nobody wanted to get involved with the girl who had cancer. To be honest, before I met your dad, I had one boyfriend, and we dated for four years. His name was Kyle."

"Wow, four years and you broke up? Why?"

"That's another story that I'm not ready to get into with you yet. I'll just say that he left me in our tiny apartment, and it wasn't too long after that I met your dad."

"Obviously, you loved Kyle if you were with him for four years," I said.

"I did love Kyle. But there's a difference between loving someone and being in love with someone. I was with Kyle out of convenience, and I didn't have anyone to guide me and tell me otherwise. He was there when my father died and he was a source of comfort, so I just stayed with him. I just wish you would have waited to have sex and talked to me about it first. This was your first time, right?"

"Yes, Mom, it was my first time, and I don't see what the big deal is. Sex isn't anything special or great. It hurt, it was awkward, and I'm feeling lousy about myself. I thought I was supposed to be glowing and feeling great. God, I can't believe I'm going to say this to you, but you and Dad must have amazing sex because you're always glowing."

She smiled at me and laughed lightly. "You want to know the truth? We do. Your father is an amazing man, in and out of the bedroom."

"Mom, stop it! That's way too much information, ew."

"Julia, you'll know when the time is right, and you'll know when you meet the man of your dreams. You're only sixteen, sweetie. You don't need the complications of a boy or a relationship in your life. You'll have plenty of time for that," she said as she kissed me on the head and got up from the bed.

"Hey, Mom," I said as she went to leave the room.

"Yes, sweetie."

"Am I still grounded?"

She tilted her head and pursed her lips. "Yeah, baby, you're still grounded."

"Can I ask you one more thing?"

"What is it, Julia?"

"Why did you come home?" I asked.

"The plane was having mechanical problems, so we never left the airport."

"Oh," I said as she walked out the door. *Just my luck.*

Chapter 6

I stayed in my room the rest of the night and thought about what my mom and I had talked about. The next morning was Sunday. Every Sunday, we had family breakfast. My mom said it was the one day of the week that we had to eat breakfast as a family. I didn't want to go downstairs because I couldn't face my dad after yesterday. There was a knock at my door and Collin told me it was time to eat. I took in a deep breath and headed downstairs. When I walked into the kitchen, I saw my dad sitting at the table, drinking his coffee, and looking at the newspaper. He didn't look up at me like he did every morning. I walked over to my mom and kissed her good morning. I avoided my dad because I didn't know how he'd react. Breakfast was silent, and it was uncomfortable. I ate my eggs and walked my plate to the sink. Before walking out of the kitchen, I stopped and turned around.

"I have homework I have to do, and I need my computer to do it."

My dad looked up at me with anger in his eyes. "You can use my computer in my office for your school work. You're not getting your laptop back."

"Dad, please, I'm sorry," I pleaded.

"Sorry isn't going to cut it this time, Julia."

"Dad, come on," Collin said.

"Stay of this, son. This has nothing to do with you. This is between my daughter and me."

I was so angry, I thought that maybe my mom would have talked some sense into him last night and he would have at least forgiven me, but I guess I was wrong. My heart was racing as I blurted out, "I wish you were never my father!"

He got up from the table and stared at me as he shook his head. "Get your ass upstairs. I don't want to see you the rest of the day or night!" he yelled.

"Don't worry about it; you won't have to," I cried as I ran up the stairs and to my room.

I threw myself on the bed and sobbed. I didn't know if I was crying because I got caught having sex or because I hurt my dad and he was disappointed in me. I needed to get out of here. I couldn't stay here anymore. I looked out my bedroom window as the clouds covered the sky. There was one place to which I needed to go. A place where I knew I could think and find some sense of peace. I packed a light bag because I didn't know if I was going to be coming back for a while. I heard my mom and Collin leave, which meant I was home alone with my dad. After getting dressed, I put my hair up in a ponytail and put on my shoes. I carefully opened the door and stepped outside my room, looking down the hallway and making sure he wasn't around. I tiptoed down the stairs to the kitchen and peeked around the corner to see if he was in there. He wasn't. I would bet he was in his office. I couldn't take the elevator out of the penthouse because he would hear the doors open, so I quietly opened the front door and stepped out, pulling it closed as softly as I could behind me. As I let out a deep breath, I took the elevator down to the lobby and left the building.

It looked like it was going to rain as I walked to Central Park, but I didn't care. Rain or shine, it was still my place of solace. I found an open spot on the grass in the Conservatory Gardens and I sat myself down, bringing my knees to chest. Tears started to fall, as did the rain from the sky. I looked up and let the raindrops hit my face while I pondered about how much my life sucked. The rain was cool as it hit my skin and I sobbed with my head buried into my knees.

"I never thought that I'd be here, doing this with my daughter," I heard a voice say from behind.

I lifted my head and looked behind me, as my dad stood a few feet away from me, holding an umbrella. "Spare me the talk, Dad. There's nothing else you can say that will hurt me more than I'm already hurting."

He walked over to me and sat down. I couldn't believe my dad was sitting on the wet grass. "I knew I'd find you here."

Being Julia

I looked at him as he handed me a small towel. "How did you know where I was?"

"This is the one place your mom would always run to after we'd have an argument. I went to your room to talk to you and you were gone." He smiled. "You're just like your mom."

"Is that a bad thing?" I asked.

"No, baby, it's not. Your mom is an amazing woman and you should be very proud to be like her."

I smiled softly at him as he took a hold of my hand. "Julia, I'm sorry for earlier and the way I yelled at you. I've done some things in my life that I'm not proud of. In fact, I've done many things that I regret, and I don't ever want you to have any regrets in life. You're my princess, and I'd do anything to protect you and make sure that you don't have any regrets."

"You can't always do that, Daddy. You're going to have to let me make mistakes because it's the only way I'll learn, and yesterday was a mistake," I said as I looked down.

He took in a sharp breath and put his arm around me, pulling me into him. "My sweet baby girl, we all make mistakes, but you're only sixteen years old. What were you thinking?"

"I was thinking about how much I wanted to be loved by someone the way you love Mom. All of my friends' parents are divorced or can't stand each other. But you and Mom, your love is like nothing I've ever seen. It's real and it's natural, and sometimes hard to believe with the things I've seen in this world. That's the kind of love I want."

"Baby, you're only sixteen. You're trying to grow up way too fast. You'll find someone who will love you like your mom and I love each other someday, when you're older. I never knew what love was until I was thirty years old, and it was the first time that I saw your mom."

I lifted my head up and looked at him. "When you saw her in the kitchen after your drunken night at the club?"

He raised his eyebrow at me. "She told you about that?"

"Yes, and she said something about a list of rules you had and how you thought she broke one of them. What's that about?"

"Nothing that you ever need to know about. The only thing you need to know is that my list of rules was one of my regrets," he said as he kissed the top of my head.

"Mom said I'll know who the right person is when he looks at me and takes my breath away."

His grip around me tightened. "She's right. You'll know it in an instant. Now, do you think we can go somewhere else and talk? It's really raining, and I'm tired of being wet."

I laughed as I pulled away from him. "Let's go home, Dad."

Being Julia

He took my hand and we walked out of the park. "I'm really sorry, Dad. I never meant to hurt you, and if I could take back the events of yesterday, I would."

"I know you're sorry, Julia," he said.

We climbed into the Range Rover and headed home. "Go upstairs and get into some dry clothes. We'll go out to lunch and stop by the store to get a new phone, since you broke yours."

"I'll pay for it. I'm sorry; it was all my fault."

"It's okay, Princess. Do you have any idea how many phones your mom has broken because of me?"

I laughed at him as we headed upstairs and went into our bedrooms to change. As soon as I changed into some dry clothes, I knocked on his door, and he told me to come in. "Are you ready, Dad?"

He sat down at the end of the bed and patted for me to come sit next to him. "I have one question, Julia, and please don't be embarrassed by it. I need to know that Brody used a condom."

Oh God, I wanted to die when I heard those words come from my father. I knew it took everything he had to ask that. "Yes, Dad, we used a condom. If it makes you feel any better, it wasn't a good experience at all, and I consider it one of my regrets."

I saw his eyes fill with tears. He put his arm around me, and I put my head on his shoulder. "Oh, sweetheart, it'll be one of the best experiences of your life when you're one hundred percent ready. I promise you," he whispered as he kissed me. "Now, let's go get some lunch. Where do you want to go?"

"The Shake Shack." I smiled. "They have the best burgers in the world!"

My dad looked at me, shook his head, and sighed. "All right, if you insist on a lunch full of grease. You certainly are your mother's daughter."

"Nah, I'm just kidding, Dad. I know how much you hate that place." I laughed. "Let's go to that restaurant where we get those really good salads."

"Now, you're talking." He smiled as we both got up from the bed.

****

The first thing we did was stop at the store to get my new phone. My dad brought my broken one with him so they could try to transfer all of my contacts and pictures. As soon as I got my new phone, we walked arm and arm down the streets of New York to the restaurant. When we arrived, we were promptly seated, and I couldn't help but notice the table of women sitting across from our table. They watched as my father strutted across the restaurant and sat down in the booth.

Being Julia

Their staring continued throughout our lunch. I told my dad that I needed to use the restroom and that I'd be right back. I watched as their eyes diverted to me when I walked by as they looked me up and down. After I used the bathroom, I walked over, sat down across from my dad, and looked at the women at the table across from us.

"Hi, do I know you?" I asked with a wide smile.

"Julia, stop," my dad said.

I got up and walked over to the table, still asking the women if I knew them. "Are you sure we haven't met before? What about him, over there?" I asked as I pointed to my dad, who was giving me an evil look.

"No, I don't believe we've met," one of the women spoke up.

"Really," I said as I put my hand on my hip and looked at each of them. "See, I thought maybe we knew each other by the way you were staring at me and my father since the moment we entered the restaurant. So, since we don't know each other, then I'm going to assume that you won't be looking our way anymore. Am I correct?"

The women looked at each other in embarrassment and then looked at me and nodded their heads. "Enjoy the rest of your lunch, ladies." I smiled as I sat down.

"Julia Rose, what the hell?"

"Daddy, please. They wouldn't stop staring so I thought maybe we had met before and I just didn't remember."

We got up from the booth and, as I walked in front of my father, I heard him apologizing to the women at the table. We stepped outside and my dad hooked his arm around my neck.

"You just wait until I catch some boys staring at you," he said in a sinister voice.

****

We entered the penthouse, and my mom came walking from the kitchen. She walked over and kissed my dad on the lips, and then put her arm around me and kissed me on my head.

"I'm glad to see the two of you worked things out." She smiled.

"Look at the phone Dad bought me," I said as I held it up to my mom.

"Nice phone, Connor," she said as she looked at him.

He shrugged his shoulders. "Julia thought it would be a good idea to say a few words to a table of women at the restaurant where we had lunch."

"Why? Were they staring at your dad?" my mom asked as she looked at me.

"Yes. They were staring at him the entire time, and then they looked me up and down, so I felt like I had to say something."

My mom high-fived me and smiled. I looked at my dad and he walked away, shaking his head while mumbling something under his breath.

"Don't you ever get tired of it, Mom?" I asked.

"Sometimes, I do. But your father is a very sexy man, so you really can't blame them for looking."

"I'm sorry, but I can't think of Daddy being a sexy man. I draw the line at handsome." I smiled.

I took my phone and went upstairs to my room. The first person I sent a text message to was London.

"Hey, I got a new phone, and I'm not grounded anymore. Why don't you come over so we can talk about yesterday?"

"OMG! Collin told me what happened, and I'm really sorry. I'll be up in a second."

After I thought about it, I ran downstairs and asked my dad if it was okay that London came over. He said it was fine and he thanked me for asking. I was relieved that my dad and I were back on good terms. He was the most important person in my life and the thought of hurting him the way I did killed me. I walked over to where he was sitting at his desk and kissed him on the cheek.

"What was that for?"

"I'm sorry for everything I said the past couple of days. I don't hate you, and I'm very happy that you're my dad."

"Julia. Thank you, baby. I love you so much," he said as he reached over and hugged me.

"I love you too, Dad." I smiled as I walked out of his office.

When I approached the kitchen, I heard London talking to my mom. I walked over and hooked my arm around her neck.

"Upstairs, now," I said.

"Yes, ma'am! See ya, Mrs. Black." She smiled.

We ran up the stairs to my room, and I shut the door as London lay down on the bed.

"So, how was it? Have you talked to him? I bet your dad almost killed him."

"You're asking way too many questions. First, it was awful, and I want my virginity back."

London turned her head and put her hand on mine. "The first time is always hard. It's like learning to ride a bike. Just get back on and try again. Eventually, you'll get it right." She smiled.

I sat up and looked at my phone. I opened up my contacts and sent a text message to Brody.

"Hi, I can't wait to see you again. Call me."

"Was he gentle?" London asked as she sat up.

"Yeah, he was, and he kept asking me if I was okay."

I looked at my phone and saw nothing. He didn't text me back yet.

"Don't worry about it, Julia. He'll text you back. He's probably busy right now."

I gave a small smile as something inside me told me that I wouldn't be hearing from him again.

Chapter 7

A couple of weeks passed and I hadn't heard a word from Brody. It was driving me crazy and I was becoming depressed over it. I headed down to the art studio, where my mom was painting a new picture.

"Hi, honey," she said.

"Hey, Mom. Can I talk to you for a minute?"

"Sure, baby," she said as she put down her paintbrush, wiped her hands, and sat down on the couch next to me.

"I haven't heard from Brody since that day."

She put her arm around me. "I was going to ask you if you'd talked to him or if you were still seeing him."

"I've called him and I've text messaged him, and he won't respond," I said as I looked down and put my head on her shoulder.

My mom sighed as she tightened her arm around me. "Sometimes, we have to learn things the hard way. The best thing to do is lift your chin up and move on. He's bad news, Julia. I know he was your first, but believe me when I tell you,

Being Julia

it's for the best. Because if you were with him, you'd be missing out on the person you were really meant to be with."

"It still hurts," I said as a tear fell down my face.

"I know it does, baby. Time heals all wounds and it's going to take time. I promise you'll start to feel better every day." She smiled as she lifted up my chin. "Now, let's go to Black Enterprises and pick up your dad so we can all go to the gym."

"Is Collin coming with us?" I asked.

"No, he's over at Hailey's house getting help in Biology."

"I bet he is." I smiled.

"Julia Rose Black. Don't talk like that!" She smiled.

We went up to the penthouse, changed our clothes, and headed over to my dad's office to pick him up. I called London and asked if she wanted to go with us, but she hadn't been feeling well lately and she said she was in bed. I was starting to worry about her because, over the past week, she wasn't acting normal, and she wouldn't tell me what was going on.

When we arrived at Black Enterprises, I could hear my father yelling from his office. I looked at my mom and she rolled her eyes.

"Great, I hope he's not in a mood." She smiled.

The minute I opened the door, he looked up at us, and threw his phone across his desk.

"Am I glad to see my favorite girls!" He smiled as he walked over to me, kissed me on the cheek, and then hugged my mom tightly.

"What was all that about, Dad?" I asked.

"Just a business deal gone bad. Nothing for you to worry about, Princess."

"All right. Are you ready to go to the gym?" my mom asked him.

"I'm more than ready to get the hell out of here." He smiled as he put his arms around both of us and we walked out of his office.

****

We walked through the doors of the gym and went to our private locker room. As soon as my dad changed his clothes, the three of us climbed on the treadmills. Most teenagers would be embarrassed to be working out with their parents, but I wasn't. I had my headphones in, listening to my music as my mind was still reeling over Brody. When my time was up on the treadmill, I stepped off, grabbed the towel from my dad's hand, and looked across the gym as Brody Sullivan was lifting weights. I gulped at the sight of him. Instead of feeling weak in the knees and butterflies, I felt rage, anger, and hostility. My skin started to heat up as I threw my towel down and stomped over to the weight bench. He was on his back, doing bench presses when I stood over him, staring down into

Being Julia

the eyes I wanted to poke out. He lifted his weight and I grabbed it. Holding it with him over his head.

"Umm... hey, Julia. How are you?"

"I'm good, Brody. How are you?"

"I'd be better if I could put this weight down."

I looked straight ahead and saw my mom and dad watching me. My dad took a step forward and my mom grabbed his arm and held him back. I helped Brody put the weight back on the bench and he sat up and looked at me as he wiped his face with a towel.

"Why haven't you called me?" I asked.

He looked down as he wiped the back of his neck. "I've been busy."

"Funny, you weren't busy when you were trying to have sex with me."

"Julia, lower your voice," he said as he stood up and looked around.

"You took something from me and then you ignore me?"

"I took what you gave. You wanted it and you were more than willing to give it up. Don't play the good little girl, Julia," he said as he started to walk away.

I grabbed him arm and stopped him. "Did you use me for sex? Did you only date me because you wanted to have sex with me?"

"Listen, Julia. You need to leave me alone. I'm not interested in you, and I'm sorry if you became attached."

I actually felt my heart break when he said that. "You didn't answer my question," I whispered.

My mom and dad walked over and my mom looked at me and then at Brody. "Hi, Brody," she said as she hooked her arm around his neck and squeezed.

"Mrs. Black, you're hurting me," he said.

"My daughter asked you a question and you will give her an answer."

He looked up at my dad, and my dad just shrugged his shoulders. "Sorry, Brody. You play, you pay. I've been there, done that and, believe me, it's not pretty. Piss off a woman and be prepared to deal with the consequences."

"Okay..okay. I only dated you to have sex with you."

My mom tightened her grip around Brody's neck after he said that. I felt like a complete fool and I wanted to cry right there. But I wouldn't give him the pleasure of seeing me break. So I did what seemed natural. I grabbed his crotch and held his royal jewels in my hand. By this time, everyone in the gym was staring.

"It's okay, Brody. Because these, right here in my hand, are nothing to be proud of."

I held up my pinky finger from my other hand in front of his face. "See this? This is your dick. Now every time you see me and I hold up this finger, you'll be reminded of how small you really are," I said as I let go of his balls.

"You're a crazy bitch. You know that?" he said.

My mom leaned closer to him and whispered, "Did you know that this is my gym? My husband bought it for me as an anniversary gift. So you better listen very carefully, Mr. Sullivan. You are never to step foot in my gym again. Because if you do, I'll charge your dumb ass with statutory rape. Have I made myself clear?"

Brody gulped as he looked at me. "Yes, Mrs. Black, I understand you," he said and then looked at my dad.

My dad shook his head slowly. "Sorry; her gym, her rules. I think you better apologize to my daughter."

"I'm sorry, Julia. I'm really sorry if I hurt your feelings," he said as my mom removed her arm from him.

"Save it for someone who cares," I said as I stuck up my pinky finger and called Bobby, our security guard, over. "Please escort Mr. Sullivan out and make sure he doesn't come back, ever."

"Sure thing, Miss Black." He smiled.

My dad walked over to me and put his arm around me. I started to break down.

"Julia, hold it together. Don't give him the satisfaction," he said as he walked me back to our locker room.

I held it in until we reached the room. As soon as the door shut behind me, I sobbed into my father's chest. He held my head against him as he told me it would be okay.

"I know it hurts, baby. Let it out."

"You...you...were right all along," I sobbed.

My mom walked over and rubbed my back. "We all make mistakes, Julia. If we didn't, we wouldn't be human. I know you're hurting, but we're here for you."

And that was what happened when I was sixteen. I lost my virginity, disappointed my parents, and I managed to get over Brody Sullivan. My mom was right; time does heal all wounds and the best way to heal those wounds: find another hot guy!

Chapter 8

Seventeen

I've dated a multitude of boys over the past year. My dad kept a careful eye on me for the fear that he'd catch me having sex in the penthouse again. My mom took me to the doctor and had me put on the pill. She told me not to mention it to my dad because he wouldn't understand. I hadn't had sex since my little romp with Brody, because of all the guys I've dated, none of them were worthy. London and I went to the mall practically every day after school. We'd sit in the food court and watch the hot guys walk by. We were on a mission, or should I say, I was on a mission to find the perfect boyfriend because London was still dating Rob, who I couldn't stand. He was only using her for her money and for sex. As much as I tried to tell her, she would just tell me that I was jealous. I was really concerned because he used drugs and, sometimes, when I'd see London with him, she looked high as hell.

I had an art competition coming up in a few days, and I needed to finish the painting that I was entering in the contest. The prize was a $15,000 scholarship to Columbia University and the winning portrait would be displayed on the wall in one of their most prestigious halls. I really wanted to go away to college, but when I mentioned it, I saw the hurt and sadness in my dad's eyes. He told me that he would support whatever decision I made. I like to tease him, so one day, I told him that I had applied to a university in Italy. He went on a rant and threw his hands up in the air; it was funny to see him get all worked up. Later that night, I overheard him talking to my mom, and he told her that if I was serious about going to Italy, then he was going to start looking for a house, and they'd live there for the next four years. I quickly told my dad that I was joking and that I wanted to go to Columbia, here in New York, so I didn't have to leave him or my home. He wrapped his arms around me and held me so tightly, I could barely breathe.

"You have no idea how happy I am that you decided to go to Columbia," he said as he kissed me on the head.

"Yeah, Dad, I think I do," I said as I tried to take a breath.

He broke our embrace and I told him I had to go down to the art studio to put the final touches on my painting. He smiled at me and told me not to stay down there too late. I loved the art studio because when I was there, it felt like my own apartment. The best part of painting at night was when the light from the moon shined into the big windows and onto my canvas. I loved sitting behind my canvas at night, painting and looking out at the brightly lit up city. One final brushstroke, and I was done. The painting for the art contest was finally finished and would be ready for submission in a few days. I looked at the clock on the wall and it was midnight. As I was cleaning up my paints and brushes, my phone rang. I looked over to where it sat on the counter and noticed it was London calling.

"Hello," I answered.

"Hey, is this London's best friend?" a strange male voice asked.

"Yeah. Who's this?"

"My name is Garrett and I think you need to come get your friend from my party. She's really strung out."

My mind was in a state of confusion as I tried to process what Garrett had just said. "Where do you live?" I asked.

He rattled off his address as I wrote it down on a piece of paper. I started to feel sick and I had no idea what to do. I couldn't get her by myself because if my parents were to check up on me, like they frequently did, I'd be grounded for life.

"Thanks. I'll be there as soon as I can."

"Please hurry. She's in really bad shape," Garrett said as he hung up.

I locked up the apartment and ran up to the penthouse. My mom and dad were sitting on the couch, watching a movie. I opened the door and my dad looked at me.

"I was just about to come down and get you," he said.

"Dad, Mom, we have to go get London. Someone named Garrett just called me and said she's at his party and she's really strung out and I need to come get her."

My mom looked at my dad and both of them got up from the couch. My dad grabbed his keys as we went down to the parking garage, and we climbed into the range Rover.

"Do you have the address?" my dad asked.

I rattled it off to him as he punched it into his GPS. My mom turned around and looked at me as I sat there on the verge of tears.

"Honey, did you know she was going to this party?" she asked.

"No. God, Mom, I hope she's okay."

"She'll be okay, sweetie," she said as she reached her hand back.

We arrived at the house and I got out of the Range Rover as soon as my dad put it in park. I ran up to the door, and when I walked in, I saw people everywhere. Couples were making out all over the house, and the stench of alcohol filled the air. I asked some of the people around who Garrett was and they told me he was upstairs in one of the rooms. My parents and I ran up the stairs and knocked on one of the doors, calling Garrett's name. Finally, the door I knocked on opened.

"Are you Garrett?" I asked.

Being Julia

"Yeah. You must be the best friend."

"My name is Julia, you idiot, and where the hell is London?"

He pointed to the bed where her half-naked body lay. She didn't have any underwear on. I ran over to her and saw that she was passed out. My mom and dad ran into the room and my mom covered her lower half with the sheet. As my dad bent down and looked at her, he yelled for us to call an ambulance.

"What did you do to her?" I screamed at Garrett as I grabbed his shirt and pushed him into the dresser.

"I didn't do anything. I found her like that. I came in here to lie down because I drank too much and she was like that. I scrolled through her phone and you were listed as her best friend, so I called you. I can't believe you brought your parents."

My mom called 911 and my dad tried to wake up London. "What did she take?" he asked as he looked at Garrett.

"Seriously, man. I don't know. Like I said, I just found her like this. When I walked in the room, she whispered something to me and then passed out."

"What did she whisper?" I asked.

"I don't know. I couldn't understand her."

"Who did she come here with?" my mom asked him.

"I don't know who he was; some older dude," he replied.

Two paramedics came through the door with a stretcher and went right over to London. They started asking a bunch of questions that we didn't have the answers to. They said her vitals were bad and they needed to get her to the hospital right away. I started shaking and crying as my dad walked over and hugged me.

"It's going to be okay, baby. We should call her parents."

"I'll call them right now," my mom said as she pulled out her phone. After several tries, she looked at us. "I can't get a hold of her mom or dad."

"Her dad is out of town on a business trip and her mom is probably passed out in some guy's bed," I said.

"Julia, that's not nice," my mom said.

"Well, it's true, Mom. I should've seen this coming. I knew she was using drugs, but she told me that she'd stop because it was messing her up."

"Please tell me you've never done drugs with her, Princess," my dad said in a panicked tone.

"No, Daddy, I've never done any drugs."

He let out a sigh of relief as we walked to the Range Rover and headed to the hospital.

****

Being Julia

We waited in the waiting room until the doctor came out and spoke to us.

"London should be fine. We sent some blood work to the lab for testing, and we pumped her stomach. I'll be honest with you; she almost died. Her test results showed her positive for cocaine, crystal meth, marijuana, and a lot of alcohol; her levels were off the charts. I would suggest you keep trying to get a hold of her parents. I've ordered a psych evaluation and she's going to have to go into a rehab program. I'm sorry this happened," the doctor said as he turned and walked away.

My mom and dad put their arms around me as the nurse took us to the room where London was. My eyes started to fill with tears when I saw her lying there. She was pale and looked like death. The beeps of the machines made me cringe, as did the smell that infiltrated the room. I walked over to her bedside and placed my hand on hers. Tears started to stream down my face as she slowly opened her eyes. She tried to talk, but she couldn't. Tears fell from her eyes as she looked at my mom and dad.

"It's okay, honey. Don't be scared," my mom said as she leaned over her and pushed her hair from her forehead.

"I'm sorry," London whispered as she looked at me.

"We can talk about it tomorrow. You need to rest now," I said to her.

London closed her eyes and turned her head. "I'll stay with her. You two go home and get some rest," my mom said. "Connor, you need to try and get a hold of Joan."

"I'll go to their apartment now," he said as he kissed my mom on the head. "Come on, Princess, let's go see if we can track down her mother and then go home," he said as he put his arm around me.

I started to walk out of the room, then I stopped and turned around and stared at my best friend, who I almost lost. I looked down as my dad pulled me closer into him and we walked out of the room. When we arrived at the building, we took the elevators up to the fifteenth floor where London's apartment was. My dad knocked on the door and London's mom surprisingly answered it.

"Connor, Julia? It's almost three a.m. What the hell is going on?"

"Didn't you get Ellery's message, Joan?"

"Message? What message?" she said as she shook her head.

Suddenly, we heard a man's voice from the other room, asking her if everything was all right. She told him to go back to sleep. The voice wasn't Mr. Fitzgerald's.

"London is in the emergency room from an overdose of drugs," my dad said.

"What? She's spending the night at her friend Ruby's house. She told me she was spending the weekend there."

Being Julia

"She lied to you, Joan. Ellery's there with her now. We both tried calling you, but you didn't answer your phone and neither did Ron."

Tears filled her eyes as she told us thank you and shut the door. My dad looked at me and shook his head. We went up to the penthouse and I grabbed a bottle of water from the refrigerator. My dad walked in behind me.

"Listen, Princess, I want you to go upstairs and go to bed. I'm going to get your mom at the hospital. I'll take you back tomorrow so you can visit London," he said as he kissed me on the head.

"Okay, Dad. I'm scared. What if–"

"No what if's, baby. She received medical attention in time and she's going to be all right," he said as he hugged me. "Now, go to bed."

"Good night, Daddy," I said as I walked away.

It didn't matter what my dad said; I was still scared and worried that London wasn't going to be okay. I knew she had been using drugs and I had tried to stop her, but I couldn't. I should've told my parents. Maybe they could've helped her before it got this far. I laid my head on my pillow and, when I closed my eyes, the only thing I saw was London's half-naked, lifeless body, lying on the bed.

A few hours later, I awoke, drenched in sweat from a nightmare I was having. I lay there as my heart was pounding.

I saw the door open from the corner of my eye and I turned my head to see Collin standing there.

"Is London going to be okay?" he asked.

"The doctor said she is," I replied.

"Good. When you go and see her, tell her I said hi." He smiled.

"I will. Are Mom and Dad up?"

"Yeah, they're in the kitchen, having coffee."

I threw back the covers, climbed out of bed, and headed downstairs to the kitchen. "Good morning." I yawned as I grabbed a cup from the cupboard.

"Morning, Princess," my dad said.

"Good morning, honey," my mom said as she kissed me on the head.

I poured coffee in my cup and sat down next to my dad.

"Did you sleep well?" he asked.

"No. I had nightmares all night," I said as I held the hot cup between my hands.

"As soon as you're ready, let me know, and I'll take you over to the hospital."

"Thanks, Dad." I smiled.

"Any time, Princess." He smiled back as he got up from his chair.

As I finished my coffee, I had a conversation with my mom and then I ran upstairs to get dressed. My dad dropped me off at the hospital and he went into the office for a while. They had moved London to up to a room on the third floor. As I stepped off the elevator, I saw her mom walking towards me.

"Hi, Mrs. Fitzgerald," I said.

"Hi, Julia," she said as she grabbed my hands. "Thank you for your help last night and for getting your parents involved. If you hadn't, London probably wouldn't be with us right now."

"I just wish I could have done something sooner," I said as I looked down.

"You did what you could and I'm grateful. I'm going to get something to eat and grab some coffee. I'll give you and London some privacy."

I smiled as I thanked her and walked away. Walking into London's room, I looked at her and she turned her head to face me.

"Hey," she said.

"Hey." I waved from the doorway.

"Save it, Julia. I know what you're going to say and frankly, I'm in no mood right now."

I walked over to her bed and sat down beside her. "You almost died. Do you even get that? Do you have any idea what it was like to find you and see you like that?"

"I'm sorry," she whispered as she turned and looked the other way.

"What happened with Rob? Wait until I get a hold of him!"

"I wasn't with Rob. I haven't seen him in a few days."

I looked at her and shook my head. "Wait a minute. Garrett said you were with some older dude. If it wasn't Rob, then who was it?"

"I don't know." She started to cry. "He was at the party and we started talking. He asked me if I liked to get high, and I told him yeah, and he took me into the bedroom and we–"

I put my hand up. "I know what you did. You got high and you had sex with him."

"I don't remember having sex," she said as she looked at me pathetically.

"You didn't have any underwear on when I walked into the room. The doctor examined you and said you recently had sex. Did he rape you?"

"I don't know." She continued to cry.

I leaned over and wrapped my arms around her, holding her tight. "You need help, London. You have to stop the drugs. Look what it's doing to you," I said as the tears began to fall.

"I know and I'm going into rehab after they release me. My mom's making the arrangements with a rehab facility in California."

Being Julia

"California? No. Why can't you go to a rehab here in New York?"

"Because the rehab facility in California is one of the best and it's only for teenagers," Mrs. Fitzgerald said as she entered the room. "I just got off the phone with them and we're all set. You'll leave the day after tomorrow."

London shook her head and began to cry again. I pulled out my phone and sent my dad a text message.

"Dad, please come to the hospital right away. I need to talk to you."

"I'm on my way, Princess," he replied.

I told London that I'd be right back, and I went and waited for my dad in the lobby. As I saw him walk through the doors, I ran up to him and threw my arms around him.

"Baby, what's wrong? Did something happen?" he asked.

"Mrs. Fitzgerald is sending London to a rehab facility in California, Dad. Please try to talk her out of it. Please!" I begged.

"Julia, I know you're upset, but it's none of our business. London is her daughter and she can make whatever decisions she wants," he said as he kissed my head and led me over to the couch to sit down.

"But, Daddy, she can go to rehab here. You can find out which one is the best and tell Mr. and Mrs. Fitzgerald. You're always finding out what's best. Please, don't let them send her away."

"Calm down, Princess," he said as he pulled me into him. "Let's go and see London and we'll take it from there."

I wiped my eyes and blew my nose with the tissue my dad handed me. I took his hand and we went up to the third floor where London was. When we walked into the room, Mrs. Fitzgerald got up from her chair and walked over to us. I could tell she always had a thing for my dad.

"Connor, it's so nice to see you again," she said as they hugged lightly.

"Hello, Joan."

I walked over to London and sat down on the edge of the bed while my dad and her mom talked.

"If you're sending London off to a rehab in California, then I'm offering you my plane and we can take the three of you to California."

"It's only going to be myself and London going. Ron is still on his business trip and he can't fly back. I can't ask you to do that, Connor," she said as she put her hand on my dad's chest.

"You're not asking, Joan. I'm insisting. In fact, since the girls won't see each other for a long time, we'll travel with you."

"Really, Dad?!" I exclaimed.

Being Julia

He looked over at me and smiled.

"If you insist, Connor, then who am I to say no to your generosity." She smiled.

Ugh. She was coming on to my dad, and I was going to have to have a talk with my mom. My dad walked over to London and kissed her forehead.

"How are you feeling, sweetheart?" he asked her.

"I'm okay, Mr. Black. Thank you."

"We're going to make sure you get the help you need so you can put this behind you and move on with your life." He smiled.

"Thank you," she said as a tear fell down her face.

****

The day had come to take my best friend to rehab. The once beautiful, dark-haired girl with the big blue eyes looked sullen and lost. I wasn't allowed to see her until we boarded the plane. Mrs. Fitzgerald said that they had too much to do to get ready for California and that she and London needed some time alone. I put my arm around her as we boarded the plane.

"How are you?" I smiled.

"Not good, Julia. As much as I'm trying to forget about the drugs, I can't, and I'm craving them so bad."

"It'll get easier. I promise. The doctors are going to help you and you're going to get better. I feel like I've let you down and I'm really sorry."

London took my hand. "You didn't let me down. You tried to get me to stop using and I did nothing but lie to you. You're the only person in my life who cares about me and I let *you* down, Julia."

My dad walked over to where we were sitting and gave London a hug. "People make mistakes, London. I know firsthand about mistakes. The people who truly love you, forgive you, and would do anything in the world to help you." He smiled.

"I wish you were my dad," she whispered.

He looked at me as he kissed her on the head. My dad was the most amazing person I knew. Collin walked over and sat with us while my dad set up his laptop on the table. I watched as Mrs. Fitzgerald walked over to him and wrapped her arms around him.

"I just can't thank you enough for doing this for us," she said.

She was just a little too close to him and, from where I was sitting, I could smell the fresh alcohol on her breath. She must've been drinking when she disappeared for fifteen minutes in the bathroom. I looked over and saw my mom staring at her. The look in her eye was one that I'd seen many times before when she was getting pissed off. My dad took Mrs. Fitzgerald's arms and removed them.

"Like I said before, Joan, I wanted to do this and you're welcome."

She took it upon herself to sit down in the chair next to him. She placed her hand on his leg and my dad looked at her. I was just about to get up and say something when I saw my mom leap out of her seat.

"Hey, Collin, Julia, why don't you take London in the back and show her the view from the window in the bedroom."

Collin and London got up and started to walk to the back bedroom.

"Are you coming?" London turned around and asked.

"Yeah, I'll be there in a second," I said.

My mom was going to let Mrs. Fitzgerald have it, and I wasn't about to miss it. She looked over at me and winked as she approached her and my dad.

"Joan, how's Ron doing?"

Mrs. Fitzgerald quickly removed her hand from my dad's leg. "He's fine, Ellery. He's on an important business trip. He's sorry that he couldn't be here."

"Really? I would imagine any father that loves his child would be there for her in her time of need," my mom said.

"It's really none of you concern, Ellery."

"See, Joan, it is my concern. It became my concern when you started trying to get my husband to sleep with you many years ago."

"I don't know what you're talking about," Mrs. Fitzgerald said as she looked away.

"Ellery, that's enough!" my dad said.

"Connor, this is between me and Joan. Butt out!"

Oh, this was getting good. My mom was letting Mrs. Fitzgerald *and* my dad have it!

My dad looked at me with that look, and I smiled. He shook his head and got up from the table. My mom continued her rant with Mrs. Fitzgerald and told her she was an alcoholic and that she needed to go to rehab as well. She also told her that she and my dad were more of a mother and a father to London over the years than she and Mr. Fitzgerald were. Mrs. Fitzgerald got up from her seat and stormed off to the bathroom. I watched as my dad walked over to my mom and looked at her with his "are you serious" look.

"Really, Ellery? Of all days to say something to Joan, you pick today?"

"She made it today the minute she put her hand on your leg. I will not apologize for telling the truth. Get over it, Connor, because you would have done the same damn thing, if not something worse, if it was Ron who put his hand on my leg."

Being Julia

My dad sighed and kissed her on the head. "I guess you're right, baby," he said as he walked away.

I laughed as I walked over to my mom. "You sure told Mrs. Fitzgerald off."

She smiled at me, tilted her head, and pushed a strand of my hair behind my ear. "Sometimes, you need to remind some people of what's yours, and yours alone."

The pilot alerted us that we were in California and to take our seats for landing. I sat down next to London and grabbed her hand. Little did I know that when I said goodbye to her at the rehab center, it would be the last time I ever saw her. She passed away right before my eighteenth birthday of a drug overdose. The rehab center could offer no explanation of how or where she got the drugs.

Chapter 9

Eighteen

I opened my eyes and turned my head as the morning sun trickled through the curtains. I reached over and grabbed my phone only to find about a hundred text messages from family and friends wishing me a happy birthday. As I smiled and tried to read each one, I set my phone face down on the bed and rolled over, wishing there was one from London. Not only was today my eighteenth birthday, but it was also my graduation day, and I'd be celebrating both without my best friend.

"Happy birthday, Princess." My dad smiled as he walked into my room, holding a single white rose.

"Thank you, Dad." I smiled as I hugged him tight.

"Breakfast is almost ready. The chefs have been here since the crack of dawn."

"I'll be down in a minute."

He looked at me as he sat on the edge of my bed and took my hand. "Today should be one of the happiest days of your life. I'm so sorry, Julia. I know it's hard with London being gone, but you have to try and enjoy the day."

"I know, Dad. I just don't understand why—"

"I know, baby. It's not for us to understand. We have to accept it and move on," he said as he pulled me into an embrace. "Now, get dressed and come downstairs for your birthday breakfast."

I gave my dad a half smile as he walked out of my bedroom. It was going to be such a busy day with graduation and my birthday, and a difficult one without London around. Every year on my and Collin's birthdays, my parents brought in caterers to put on a big breakfast buffet for our family and friends. After graduation ceremony, my parents were throwing me a birthday party to celebrate my birthday. My mom went wild with throwing me a graduation party at the beach house next weekend. My dad wanted it at the Astoria, but my mom said she wanted to keep it fun and casual and that we were already having my birthday party there. After I put on my sundress, I went downstairs, where everyone was sitting in the dining room, having breakfast.

"Happy birthday, Julia!" everyone yelled when I walked in.

Hailey looked at me and smiled as I walked over to her chair and hugged her.

"I know this is hard for you, but if you need anything, please let me know," she whispered.

"Thank you, Hailey."

I continued to make my rounds to each guest as I was hugged and kissed to death. I grabbed a plate and walked over to where the buffet was set up. "Happy birthday, sis," Collin said as he put his arm around me and kissed my cheek.

"Thanks, buddy."

"Maybe tomorrow, we can hang out at Central Park." He smiled.

"Yeah, maybe we can."

I made my way down the buffet table, filling my plate while faking a smile. It just didn't seem right without London here. We had a nice breakfast with conversation, laughter, and good food. After breakfast was finished, everybody went home until the graduation ceremony. I was on my way upstairs when my mom and dad called me into the living room. My mom had her hands behind her back with a smile on her face.

"Happy birthday, sweetheart." She smiled as she handed me a small red velvet box. "We wanted to give this to you now instead of at the party tonight."

I sat down on the couch in between my parents and slowly lifted the lid. Inside sat a beautiful diamond infinity ring. It was stunning and I loved it.

"Mom, Dad," I said as I looked at it with tears in my eyes.

"You know by now that symbol has a special meaning in our family. We wanted to give you something that represents us as a family; something you can look at when your dad and I are gone and know that our love for you is forever, even when we're not here," my mom said.

"Thank you so much. I love it," I said as I hugged them both. "I'll never take this ring off."

"I'm glad you like it, Princess. Your mom and I thought it would be the start of a tradition. You can pass it on to your daughter when she's eighteen."

"What if I don't have a daughter?"

"Well, let's hope you do." He smiled.

I went upstairs, showered, and dressed for my graduation ceremony. It felt unreal that I was finally out of school and going to college in the fall. I put on my graduation gown and stood in front of my full-length mirror as I put my graduation cap on my head. There was a soft knock on door and my mom peeked her head in.

"Do you need any help?" she asked.

"No. I think I got it."

She stepped into my room and walked up behind me, clasping my shoulders with her hands.

"I can't believe that my baby girl is graduating. It seems like it was only yesterday that I took you to your first day of preschool."

"You're going to make me cry," I said as I looked at her through the mirror.

"Time goes by so fast, Julia. It's important to cherish every day," she said as she straightened my cap and patted my shoulders. She walked out of the room just as my dad walked in, smiling at me.

"My princess is graduating high school. It's amazing how fast the time went. I'll never forget your first day of kindergarten." He smiled.

I turned around as he sat down on the bed. "I had my arms wrapped tightly around your leg and I wouldn't let go."

"That's right." He smiled as he reached for my hand and asked me to sit down. "You were so scared and you held onto me as if your life depended on it."

"I begged you not to leave me." I smiled.

"And I didn't. I promised you that I wouldn't leave, so I sat in the back of the classroom to make sure you were okay. Just like I'll be sitting in the audience, making sure you're all right when you accept London's diploma and give your speech."

The tears I tried so hard to hold back started to fall. My dad reached over and gently wiped them away with his finger. "No tears, baby. You'll ruin your makeup."

"Thanks, Dad," I said as I laid my head on his shoulder.

****

Being Julia

As I stood at the podium and looked at my notes, I looked out into the audience and saw my parents sitting in the second row. My mom blew me a kiss and my dad gave me a thumbs up. I was nervous and started to sweat. I folded the white piece of paper I had in my hand and pushed it to the side. I gripped the sides of the podium, took in a deep breath, and closed my eyes as I began to speak into the microphone. I spoke about the last four years, London, and her death. I could hear the sounds of sniffling as I talked about what an amazing student and person London was. A tear fell from my eye as I read my closing statement and I received a standing ovation, not only for my speech, but because my painting won the art competition and I was the recipient of a $15,000 scholarship to Columbia.

I walked off the stage and took my seat with my fellow classmates as they wiped their tears. It was time for the distribution of diplomas and when London's name was called, I proudly walked across the stage and accepted her diploma for her. I kissed it and held it up the air, with the hope that she was looking down and could see it. Once the ceremony was over, I met my family out in the lobby. My mom started to cry as she hugged me tightly, while my dad was grinning from ear to ear. As soon as my mom let me go and my dad wiped the tears from her eyes, Collin hugged me and told me that he was proud that I was his sister. After I made my rounds and hugged my entire family, Mason walked over to me with tears in his eyes.

"Princess, you were amazing up on that stage. I'm so proud of you." He began to cry as he hugged me tightly and had a full breakdown.

I looked at my dad and he rolled his eyes. He tapped my mom on the shoulder and pointed to Uncle Mason. My mom turned around and smiled at me as she clasped his shoulders and broke our embrace.

We left the graduation and went straight to the Astoria for my birthday party. There were around 150 guests that showed up, including family and friends from school. The room was decorated with balloons in pink and lavender, my two favorite colors. Beautiful candle lit, floral centerpieces sat in the middle of each table. There was a DJ, and a table that sat in the corner with a birthday cake that represented my shopping addiction and tiers upon tiers of beautiful flowered cupcakes. I took in a deep breath as I put on my fake smile and thanked everyone for coming. My mom ran over to me.

"Here comes your dad. I know that look on his face and it's about your dress. I'm just giving you a heads up."

"Thanks, Mom." I sighed.

My dad walked over to me and kissed me on the cheek as he put his hand on the small of my back.

Being Julia

"Happy birthday, baby. You look gorgeous. Did you pick out that dress yourself?"

"Thank you, Daddy, and yes, I did. Isn't it the most beautiful dress you've ever seen? I love it so much, and I feel like such a princess in it. Tell me you like it, Daddy, please."

Yes, that was me putting on the innocent act for my father to try and distract him from telling me that my dress was way too short. He looked at me, paused, and then smiled. "It's beautiful, Julia, and it looks wonderful on you."

"Thanks, Dad." I smiled as he started to walk away.

He stopped, turned around, and looked at me. "Your mom said something to you, didn't she?"

I shrugged my shoulders as I flashed him a smile. He turned around and shook his head. My poor dad; at least he had Collin.

Chapter 10

We packed up everything we needed for the summer and drove to the beach house. As we walked through the door, I took my suitcases upstairs to my bedroom and laid them on the bed. The first thing I did was open my window to let the ocean breeze blow through. I ran down the stairs, out through the door, nearly knocking my dad over, and down to the beach. The minute my toes hit the sand, I felt like I was home. The beach was my place of solace here, like Central Park was back in the city. Collin came running down the beach with his surfboard and hit the water. I tried to surf once, but it just ended up being a disaster. As I stood at the shoreline, the water came up and soaked my feet. I ran back up to the house to grab my sketchpad and pencil. When I walked into the kitchen, my mom was sitting up on the counter with her legs wrapped around my dad's waist as he had his hand up her shirt and they made out.

"You two seriously need to stop it!" I exclaimed.

"Julia, I thought you were down at the beach," my dad said as he instantly removed his hand from under my mom's shirt.

Being Julia

"I just came back to get my sketchpad. If you're going to have sex, please do it in your room with the door closed. You have no idea how much you've scarred me. To think of my parents having sex is just gross!"

My mom started to laugh and my dad stood there and looked at me in shock. I started to walk away and I heard my mom yell, "Just you wait, young lady. You'll find out what it's like to have the love of your life and want to make love to him every day."

"Ellery, don't tell her that," my dad said.

I smiled as I grabbed my sketchpad from my room and stopped in the doorway of the kitchen. My parents were kissing and smiling at each other. As I quietly watched them, I prayed what my mom said would come true for me one day. As I made my way back down to the beach, I sat on the sand, brought my knees to my chest, and placed my sketchpad on them. I began drawing the outline of London's face. She would come to the beach house every summer with us and we would sit together on the sand for hours. I looked up as Collin walked over to me and sat down. He was soaking wet, so I threw him his towel.

"Thanks, sis. Whatcha drawing?"

"London. I'm drawing a portrait of London."

"I know you miss her and so do I. Can I talk to you about something?"

"Sure; you can talk to me about anything," I said as I continued to draw.

"Hailey and I had sex last night."

My pencil stopped on the pad as I slowly turned my head and looked at my almost seventeen-year-old brother. "And?" I asked.

He smiled as he looked down and started drawing in the sand. "It was amazing."

"How did Hailey feel?"

"She loved it. You know, it wasn't her first time."

"Yeah, I know." I smiled as I bumped my shoulder into his.

"Where did you guys do it?"

"Her house."

"Ah, while Peyton and Henry were out to dinner with Mom and Dad."

"Yeah. We knew they'd be gone forever, so we weren't worried."

"I hope you used a condom?"

"Of course I did. I'm not stupid."

I put my pencil down and hooked my arm around his neck. "Congratulations, baby brother, on successfully losing your virginity and thinking it was amazing."

"Please don't tell Mom and Dad."

"Are you kidding me? I would never tell them. Anyway, they're too busy having sex in the kitchen to notice what's going on around them."

"Ugh, again? Those two never stop." Collin laughed.

He got up and went back to the house while I finished my drawing of London. A while later, I walked up to the house and, when I stepped into the kitchen, all I could smell was Italian food. It was the aroma of my favorite Italian take-out place called Tivoli's. They made the best pasta and sauce on the face of the Earth and their garlic bread was to die for.

"Oh, honey, I'm glad you're back. Could you set the table please?" my mom asked.

"Is it time to eat now?" I asked as I grabbed the plates from the cupboard.

"Yes, and we ordered your favorite." She smiled.

As I set the table, my mom picked up my sketchpad and looked at it. "This is beautiful, Julia."

"Thanks. I drew it while I was down at the beach."

My dad and Collin walked in, and my mom showed my dad the sketch of London.

"That's a beautiful picture, Princess," he said as he kissed me on the head.

"Thanks, Dad," I said as I grabbed the bowl of pasta and set it on the table.

We sat down and ate dinner as a family, reminiscing of the days when we were younger. Little did I know that tomorrow would be the day that changed my life forever.

****

I awoke to a whole lot of noise going on downstairs. As I yawned, I grabbed my phone and texted Collin to come to my room. He opened the door and stepped inside.

"What?" he asked.

"What the hell is going on downstairs?"

"Did you forget that today is your graduation party and the caterers and planners are here?"

"Already? My God, it's only eight o'clock in the morning."

Collin shrugged his shoulders and walked out of the room. I stepped out of bed and walked down the hallway to my parents' room. I knocked on the door and my dad told me to come in. He was sitting up on the bed, checking his phone.

"Good morning, Princess." He smiled.

"Morning, Dad," I said as I cuddled up next to him. He put his arm around me and kissed my head.

"Is something wrong?"

I sighed. "No, I just don't want to go downstairs yet with all that racket going on."

"Ah, me neither. That's why I'm sitting in here."

"Mom's okay with that?"

Being Julia

"I told her I was running up here to change clothes. She'll realize it soon enough and come look for me."

"I miss London, Dad."

"I know you do, sweetheart. We all miss London, and I know it's hard for you without her being here. But, today's your graduation party and there's going to be about 300 people here, so you need to try and at least act happy. I know you've been doing that a lot lately, but once today is over with, you'll have the whole summer to relax."

Suddenly, the door opened and my mom stood in the doorway, staring at us. "Good morning, sweetheart. Connor, why are you sitting up here?"

"I'm comforting our daughter, Ellery."

She glared at him with knitted eyebrows as she walked over to the bed. "Are you okay, sweetheart?"

"I'm fine, Mom."

"Connor, downstairs! Julia, why don't you go take a shower and get ready for your party?" She smiled.

I sat up and looked at my dad as he winked at me. As soon as I walked out of the room and shut the door, I heard giggling. I rolled my eyes because I knew what that meant.

****

The party was a success, and I could tell how happy my mom was. People were everywhere. Tables filled the patio and backyard under the beautiful white canopy tents. The spread of food was amazing and could probably feed a small country. The DJ was awesome and played everything my friends requested. My mom had a play area set up for the smaller children and then games were set up down on the beach for the older kids and adults. I made my rounds and tried to talk to as many people as I could. It was nearing dusk and I needed to step away from the party for a while to gather my thoughts. With as many people that were here to celebrate my graduation, it still felt lonely without London. I didn't want my parents to worry if they couldn't find me, and I didn't see my mom, so I told my dad I was going for a walk.

"Dad," I said as I pulled him aside. "I'm going to go for a walk down the beach in case you're looking for me."

"All right, sweetheart, just be careful," he said as he kissed my head.

I took off my shoes and headed down the beach. Once I made my way down, far enough away from the house, I sat down in the warm, soft sand. As I was thinking about my life and college, a dog came up and sat down next to me with a stick in its mouth.

"Hi there." I smiled as I reached my hand over to pet the dog. "You're so cute. Look at that face. Where did you come from?"

Suddenly, I heard a voice from a few feet away. "Mozart, there you are. What are you doing, boy?"

I gulped as I looked at the fine male that was standing in front of me, in just a pair of cargo shorts and no shirt. I couldn't help but stare at his ripped abs and muscular arms. It felt like I couldn't get enough air as I looked at him. My eyes finally traveled up to his face and, once again, my airway felt constricted. He was the hottest guy I'd ever seen in my life.

"Sorry about that. Mozart loves girls and, when he sees one, he wants to be friends." He smiled.

That smile. I felt something when he smiled. It was the kind of smile that no matter how bad your day was, it made you feel better. It was the kind of smile that fixed you. I needed to speak, but the words weren't coming out. I was stunned by this boy, this guy, this man. He had me speechless and that was not easy to do.

"That's okay. I love dogs." I managed to spit out.

He looked at me and cocked his head. "I know this is your typical crappy line, but I'm serious. I feel like we've met before."

I laughed because at least he was being honest about it being a typical crappy line. "I don't think so."

"Come on, Mozart, let's go," he said.

Mozart looked at me, laid down, and put his head on my lap.

"Mozart, what are you doing? Come on. Come, boy."

"He obviously doesn't want to go," I said.

"He never acts like this. He always listens when I tell him we have to go."

I felt my heart beating rapidly as the nervousness in my stomach began. "You could always stay for a while until he's ready to go."

He looked at me with a smile. "You don't mind? You sort of look like you want to be alone."

"No, I don't mind. I was just escaping the craziness of my graduation party."

He sat down next to me and all I could think about was running my hand down his torso, feeling every crevice and well-defined muscle he had. "Ah, I remember my graduation party last year. My parents went all out. By the way, I'm Jake Jensen." He smiled as he held out his hand.

"Nice to meet you, Jake Jensen. I'm Julia Black." I smiled back as I shook his hand.

The feeling of my skin heating up when I touched him was unreal. It was a feeling that I'd never felt in my eighteen years of living.

"It's a pleasure to meet you, Julia Black. So, why are you trying to escape your graduation party?"

Being Julia

I felt instantly comfortable with Jake, and I didn't seem to have any reservations about telling him my problems. "My best friend died a month ago from a drug overdose while she was in rehab."

"Wow. How do you overdose in rehab?"

"I don't know. Neither the doctors nor the facility could give us an explanation. She used to come here and stay with us every summer, and not to have her here, especially at my graduation party, is really hard."

"I'm really sorry, Julia," he said as he looked down.

"Thank you, but it's okay. It's all just a bit overwhelming. Enough about me. Tell me about you, Jake Jensen."

He laughed as he looked up at me. "My parents just bought the house down the beach. I have two sisters, and I just finished my first year at Columbia."

"Columbia? I'm going to Columbia in the fall." I smiled.

"Really? You'll love it, and now you know someone who can show you around."

"That's great; then, I won't feel so scared," I said as I looked down.

"No, you won't," he whispered.

I looked over at him and, for a moment, we stared into each other's eyes.

"Julia," I heard Collin yell from a distance. "Dad said you need to come back now."

"That's my brother. I guess I have to go," I said as I stood up.

"It was great to meet you, Julia Black. I hope to see you around." He smiled.

I smiled back at him as I put my hand up and gave him a small wave. I started to walk towards Collin, stopped, and turned around. "Hey, Jake," I yelled. "Would you like to come back with me so you can see the craziness of my graduation party?

He smiled as shouted back. "Sure, just let me take Mozart home and grab a shirt. I'll be back in a minute."

"I'll wait for you." I smiled. "Collin, tell Dad that I'll be there in a minute."

Collin walked over to where I was standing. "Who's that?"

"Someone who just swept me off my feet," I said as I put my head on Collin's shoulder.

Chapter 11

As I waited for Jake to return, Collin went back to the house. I stared out into the ocean as I whispered, "London, did you see him? Jake Jensen? I know I've only known him for about thirty minutes, but I think he's something special."

"Hey," Jake said as he walked up to me. "Thanks for waiting."

"Hi. No problem," I said as we walked through the sand back to my house.

We could hear the music and the laughter as we walked towards the house. "My God, how many people did your parents invite?"

"About 300 people." I smiled.

"Seriously?"

"Yeah, me and my dad were trying to hide out this morning, but my mom caught us."

We walked up to the patio and made our way through the crowd. I saw my mom standing in the kitchen, talking to my dad. Both of them turned and looked at me as we stepped through the door.

"Where have you been?" my mom asked.

Sandi Lynn

"I told Dad that I was taking a walk down the beach."

"Yes, you did, Julia, but that was a long time ago," my dad said as he looked at Jake. "Who's your friend, Princess?"

"Dad, Mom, this is Jake Jensen. We met on the beach."

Jake held out his hand to both my mom and dad. "Jensen," my dad said as he looked at Jake.

"Daddy!" I exclaimed.

"You wouldn't happen to be William Jensen's son, would you?"

"Yes, sir. He's my dad." Jake smiled.

"Ah, I knew it. Jake's father owns the largest dealership in the city, where I buy my Range Rovers. I've been buying from your father for years."

"Mr. Black, that's right. I've heard your name before. You own Black Enterprises. My dad talks about you."

"All good, I hope."

"Of course." Jake smiled.

Okay, this was perfect. My dad knew Jake's dad and he seemed to really like him. I couldn't have asked for this meeting to be more perfect.

"You and Julia have already met," my dad said.

"What? How?" I asked.

"Back when you were about eight years old and I bought a new Range Rover. You wanted to come with me to the dealership and Jake was there. He was sitting behind his father's desk. The dealership had a playroom and your father asked you to take Julia and show her the toys while we went over the numbers for the purchase."

"See, I told you I felt like we'd met before," Jake said as he smiled at me.

I wished I would have remembered that, but I didn't. Jake and my dad continued to talk while my mom pulled me into the living room.

"Oh my God, Julia. He's hot." She smiled.

"He took my breath away, Mom."

"Sweetheart." She smiled as she put her hand on the side of my face. "I don't know what to say except 'be careful.'"

I smiled at her as she placed her arm around me and we walked back into the kitchen. Jake turned around and flashed me a smile.

"Mr. Black, would it be all right with you and Mrs. Black if I took Julia on a date?"

I looked at my mom and she was grinning from ear to ear. My dad looked at me and then back at Jake before giving his answer.

"Yes, Jake. You may take my daughter on a date." He smiled as he put his hand on Jake's shoulder.

Jake walked over to me as his amazing green eyes stared into mine. "Julia, I know we've only known each other a couple of hours, but I was hoping you would do me the honor of going on a date with me tomorrow night."

I was so excited that I wanted to scream "yes!" and jump up and down, but I remained calm and smiled at him as I nodded my head and told him yes. He continued to smile at me as he nodded his head like he was happy with my answer. The fact that he asked my parents first scored him big points. As the guests were starting to leave, Jake said that he should get going. When I walked him down to the beach, he pulled his phone from his pocket and asked me for my number. I gave it to him and he told me that he'd text me so that I would have his.

"Goodnight, Julia Black. I'm looking forward to our date tomorrow night. How about I pick you up around seven o'clock?"

"Seven o'clock is perfect." I smiled.

He leaned closer to me, kissed me lightly on the cheek, and began to walk away. I called his name and he turned around. I put my hand up and gave him a small wave.

"Goodnight, Jake Jensen." I smiled.

"Sweet dreams, Julia," he said as he turned back and walked down the beach.

I said goodbye to the last guest and closed the door. I leaned up against it and sighed. My mom walked over to me and smiled.

"What a great party, but I'm glad it's over."

"Me too, Mom. Thank you for everything."

"Aw, you're welcome, sweetheart," she said as she hugged me.

I went upstairs and started a hot bath. I twisted my hair up, set my phone on the edge of the tub, and climbed in. I slid down until my head rested comfortably on the bath pillow. As I closed my eyes, the sweet smile of Jake Jensen filled my head. I couldn't help but think of his almost six foot height and his light brown, tousled hair, which made him even sexier. The shape of his lips and the smile that came from them. A smile that made his green eyes light up and captivate me when he looked into mine. As I was dreaming about Jake, my phone beeped. I opened my eyes and looked over to see a text message from him. My heartbeat picked up pace as I read his message.

"Hi, Julia. It's me, Jake. I just wanted to say goodnight and that I can't wait until our date tomorrow night."

I smiled because I couldn't wait either. I dried off my hands and quickly responded.

"Hi, Jake. I'm very excited for our date. I can't wait to see you again."

I stepped out of the tub and changed into my pajamas. I looked at the clock and it was two a.m. I walked downstairs to get a glass of water and I saw my dad sitting on the couch in the living room.

"Dad, it's late. Why aren't you in bed?" I asked as I sat down next to him.

"I'll be heading upstairs soon, Princess. Shouldn't you be in bed? You've had a long day."

"I just came down for a glass of water," I said as I sat down next to him.

"I want you to know that I like Jake and I approve." He smiled as he put his arm around me.

"I like Jake too, and I'm glad you approve. But you do know that even if you didn't approve, it wouldn't have mattered.

"I know," he sighed. "The women in my family are very defiant."

"That's because we don't like to be controlled, Mr. Black," my mom said as she entered the room. "There's only one place where I let you control me." She winked.

My dad got up from the couch and put his hands on my mom's hips. "Would you like me to control you right now?" he asked with a smile.

"Oh my God! I'm going to bed!" I exclaimed as I got up and ran up the stairs before I could hear any more.

Being Julia
****

I couldn't sleep, so I got up and started making our family Sunday breakfast. My mom and dad walked into the kitchen just as I started to make the eggs.

"Good morning, Princess. What's all this?" my dad asked as he kissed me on the head.

"I couldn't sleep, so I thought that I'd make breakfast today."

"Morning, baby," my mom said sleepily as she kissed me.

"Morning, Mom. Can you go wake up Collin?"

My dad poured some coffee and sat down at the table. "Why couldn't you sleep? Were you thinking about Jake?"

I turned to him and smiled. "Maybe."

Collin and my mom walked into the kitchen. Collin looked so tired. "You look tired," I said as I poured him some coffee.

"Gee, maybe if I wasn't kept up all night, I wouldn't be so tired. Let me tell the two of you something," Collin said as he looked at our parents. "I can appreciate how much you two love each other, but you're old and you have sex like you're in your twenties. When you bought this house, you obviously didn't consider the bedroom situation because my room is right next to yours and you don't seem to care whether I can hear you or not. I'm asking you to please add on another bedroom to the house, preferably way on the other side of where my bedroom is."

I stood there, with the spatula in my hand, in shock at what my brother had just said to our parents. My mom and dad looked at each other and then at Collin.

"Okay, son. We'll add on another bedroom," Dad said.

"That's a great idea, Collin. I'm surprised we haven't thought about it before." Mom smiled.

"You know, Ellery, the family will only grow, so maybe we should just expand the house with more than just a bedroom. Think about it. Julia and Collin will get married someday and have kids of their own, and we'll want them here in the summer to visit, so we need to make sure we have the room."

"I agree, Connor, and I think we should do it."

"Oh, Dad," I said. "There's something I've been meaning to talk to you about. It's about that scholarship I won. We don't need it, and there are students out there that do. Can we give the scholarship to someone else? To someone who really needs it?"

"I already thought of that, and I left a message for the dean. I don't see why not, and if we can't, I'll just match the scholarship and give it to someone in need."

"Thanks, Dad." I smiled as I got up from the table.

I started to clean up, but my mom told me to go and get dressed because she was taking me shopping for a new outfit for my date with Jake. It was unexpected and I was so excited.

Being Julia

She and my dad cleaned up, Collin went back to bed, and I went to my room and got dressed. As I was brushing my hair, my phone beeped with a text message from Jake.

"Good morning. I hope you slept better than I did. I can't wait to see you later. Have a great day, Julia."

"Good morning, Jake. I didn't sleep at all. I just got done making breakfast for my family and now me and my mom are going shopping."

"You cook? You're even more perfect than I thought."

My heart melted when he said that I was perfect. This feeling that had overtaken me was something I couldn't describe. I'd never felt anything like it.

"Don't put me on that pedestal yet. I can only manage to cook breakfast foods."

"I've already put you up on that pedestal, Julia. I'll talk to you later, my dad is calling me."

"Bye, Jake."

My mom and I went into the city and shopped all day. She told me that it would make the day go by faster for me and she was right. As we were leaving Starbucks, I ran right into a guy as he was coming in.

"Oh my God, I'm so sorry. I didn't see you," I apologized.

"No, it's—Ellery?" he asked.

"Kyle?" She smiled as she gave him a hug. "It's nice to see you. Wow, it's been what? At least ten years?"

"Yeah, I think so. It's good to see you, Ellery. This beautiful girl must be Julia?"

"Yes, this is my daughter, Julia. Julia, this is Kyle. We used to date."

"I would call it more than dating. We lived together for four years." He smiled.

It suddenly hit me. This was the guy my mom had talked about. He was her ex-boyfriend. "It's nice to meet you." I smiled.

"Oh boy, Elle, she has your smile."

"How have you been?" she asked him.

"I'm okay. I'm VP of the accounting firm and I've just ended my second marriage."

"Oh, I'm sorry to hear that."

"Nah, don't be. I just haven't found the right woman to spend the rest of my life with yet," he said as he looked at her with sad eyes.

She put her hand on his arm. "You will, Kyle. She's out there somewhere."

"I think I already lost her," he said as he stared into her eyes.

"Mom, look at the time. We need to get going."

Being Julia

"You're right, sweetie. It was good seeing you, Kyle. Good luck with everything."

"Thanks, Elle. It was great seeing you too. It was nice to meet you, Julia." He smiled.

As we began to walk away, Kyle called my mom's name.

"How's Connor?" he asked.

She turned around and gave him the biggest smile. "Connor is wonderful."

"Good. Tell him I said hi."

We continued walking down the street, stopping into one more store before heading home.

Chapter 12

I sat down at my vanity and put on my makeup. There was a knock on the door and my dad asked if he could come in.

"I just wanted to let you know that I spoke with the Dean of Columbia and he said it wouldn't be a problem to give the scholarship to someone else as a donation."

"That's great news, Dad. Oh, by the way, mom's ex-boyfriend, Kyle, said to tell you hi."

"What?" he asked. "When did you see him?"

"Today, while we were in the city. I ran smack dab into him as we were leaving Starbucks."

My dad sat down on my bed. "What else did he have to say?"

"Not much. He said he had just ended his second marriage. I'm pretty sure he still has a thing for Mom because he said he thinks he already lost the girl he was supposed to be with or something like that. I don't know; he seemed kind of weird."

"He never got over your mother, and I don't think he ever will."

"Why did they break up?" I asked as I was putting on my eye shadow.

"Because your mom was sick and wouldn't get the help she needed, so he left her. Which I'm thankful for, because I never would have met her if he didn't."

"Sick, how?" I asked in confusion.

"Your mom's cancer had returned when she was twenty-three years old, and she refused to get treatments because she didn't want to go through it again."

I stopped what I was doing and turned around. "What? So you mean she was going to let herself die?"

"Yes, and when Kyle found out, he left her."

"It was because of your dad that I ended up getting the treatments I needed," my mom said as she walked into the room and sat down next to my dad. He grabbed her hand and kissed it.

"Mom, what the hell were you thinking?!" I exclaimed.

"I wasn't thinking clearly, but your dad helped me with that."

"We helped each other." He smiled.

"Listen, Julia, you finish getting ready for your date. We'll discuss this another time," she said as she got up from the bed. She took my dad by the hand and led him out of my room.

I was stunned by what my father told me. I knew she had cancer when she was sixteen, but I had no idea that it came back when she was twenty-three. There was so much about my parents that I didn't know and it bothered me. I finished putting on my makeup and curling my hair. I put on the cute maxi dress my mom had bought for me, and I headed downstairs.

"Now that's the kind of dress I like to see on you." My dad smiled.

"Very funny, Dad!"

"No, seriously. That dress looks beautiful on you."

Collin came running down the stairs. "Hey, sis, you look great! Dad, we need to talk about that car you said you'd buy me."

"I know, Collin, and we will."

"But I need one now. I can't even pick up Hailey for a date because we're here at the beach house and I have no way to get to her," he said.

My dad reached in his pocket and threw his keys to Collin. "Take the Range Rover. Your mother and I aren't going anywhere tonight."

"Thanks, Dad!" Collin exclaimed as he turned around and quickly ran out the door.

"Connor, I thought we were going out to dinner?" my mom said as she looked at him.

Being Julia

He walked over to her and whispered something in her ear. Suddenly, she started grinning from ear to ear. I rolled my eyes and shook my head. I'm sure it had something to do with sex since they were going to be home alone.

There was a knock at the door and my mom said she'd answer it. I walked out of the kitchen with my dad following behind, and smiled when I saw Jake standing there. He looked at me and I pretty much stopped breathing. His face lit up when he saw me and, when I walked over to him, he took my hand and kissed my cheek. My heart was pounding so fast, there was no way he couldn't have heard it.

"You look beautiful, Julia."

"Thank you. You look amazing." I smiled.

"Are you ready to go?" he asked.

"Yes."

My dad walked up to me, kissed me on the cheek, and then shook Jake's hand. "Have fun, you two."

"What time should I have her home?" Jake asked.

"She doesn't have a curfew and just a reasonable time is fine," my mom said as she pushed us out the door before my dad could say something. "Have fun and be safe," she said and quickly shut the door.

He opened the passenger door to his Range Rover and I smiled. It was just like my dad's, but his was white. "Is this yours?" I asked him when he climbed in.

"Yeah, my parents gave it to me as a graduation present."

"Very nice!" I grinned.

"Is there anything special you want to do? Because I'll do anything you want. That is, after we grab something to eat. I'm starving."

I didn't care what we did. As long as I was with him, it didn't matter. We could sit in the Range Rover all night and listen to music and I'd be happy. "It doesn't matter to me what we do," I said.

"Do you like Italian food?"

"I love it!" I smiled.

"I know this great restaurant called—"

"Tivoli's!" we both said at the same time.

He looked at me with a wide grin across his face. "You know it?"

"It's my favorite Italian restaurant."

"Seriously? You're serious?"

"Yes, I'm serious." I laughed.

We pulled into the parking lot and Jake parked the Range Rover. He looked over at me and told me to wait while he got out. He walked around and opened the door for me.

"I will always open the door for you." He smiled as he took my hand and helped me out.

"Thank you."

Being Julia

We walked into the restaurant and it was packed. People were standing everywhere, waiting for a table. "Man, look at this line. Hold on; let me ask how long the wait is."

Jake walked back, shaking his head. "They said it's at least an hour wait. Is that okay with you or would you rather go somewhere else?"

"Come with me." I smiled as I took grabbed his hand and led him through the line of people. We walked up to the hostess desk where the manager, Alan, was standing.

"Good evening, Miss Black. Are you dining with us tonight?"

"Hi, Alan. Yes. It's just me and Jake tonight." I smiled.

"Very good. This way to your table," he said as he grabbed two menus.

We were seated at our table and Jake looked at me with a half a smile on his face. "How?"

"Welcome to the Black family's table," I said as I raised my hands. "My dad bought this table so we would never have to wait. He's crazy like that."

"That's awesome. Remind me to thank your father." Jake smiled. "Are you going to open your menu or do you already know what you're having?"

"I get the same thing every time I come here, chicken parmesan. It's the best I've ever had."

"I've never had the chicken parmesan from here; I usually get the lasagna."

The waitress came over and took our order. I smiled when Jake ordered the chicken parmesan.

"Don't hold me responsible if you don't like it." I laughed.

"If you say it's great, then I'm sure it is." He winked.

I had to stop and think for a moment because suddenly I realized that I was no longer nervous around Jake. I was comfortable and felt like I could just be myself. We talked about our families and Columbia.

"What are you studying at Columbia?" I asked.

"Corporate Finance," he said as he took a sip of his water.

I placed my hand on the table while I picked up the glass with my other hand. "Sounds interesting. You and my dad will have a lot to talk about." I smiled.

Jake looked at me and then at my hand. "I really want to hold your hand. Would that be okay? I don't want to overstep."

"You're not overstepping and I would like that."

He reached his hand over and placed it on top of mine. His skin was soft, and his touch sent a warm sensation throughout my body. He was so polite and such a gentlemen.

"What about you? What are you going to be studying at Columbia?"

"Architecture and design with a background in marketing." I smiled.

"That's an excellent field."

"I'm an artist, but I don't want to make a career out of it like my mom. So, I opted to put my talents somewhere else. Plus, I'm hoping to work for my dad at Black Enterprises. He's already grooming me and Collin to take over when he retires."

"You're an artist? Like in painting?" he asked.

"Yeah, I paint pictures. In fact, my painting just won Columbia's Art Competition. It's going to be hanging in one of the halls there."

Jake lifted my hand and interlaced our fingers. "Julia, that's amazing. I would love to see your artwork."

The waitress set our plates down in front of us and Jake cut into his chicken. He held his fork up and smiled. "Here it goes." He tilted his head to the side as he chewed with a grin on his beautiful chiseled face. "You're right. This has to be the best chicken parmesan I've ever eaten."

After we finished our dinner and shared a dessert, Jake walked around, pulled out my chair, and took my hand in his as we walked out of the restaurant. Touching him, I felt connected, and being with him made me forget about everything else in the world. He opened the door to the Range

Rover and before I climbed in, he gently placed his hand on my cheek. He smiled at me as he slowly shook his head.

"This is crazy."

"What's crazy?" I smiled.

"This feeling I have when I'm with you, when I look at you, and when I touch you."

"The same feeling I have when I'm with you."

"Really? You have it too?" he said as he inched his face closer to mine.

"I sure do." I smiled as I looked at his lips.

"You're so beautiful, Julia, and I really want to kiss you."

"I want you to kiss me," I whispered.

His smile widened as he leaned in even closer and his lips softly brushed against mine. His hand cupped the back of my head as his lips pressed firmly, forcing me to part my lips. He slipped his tongue inside my mouth and I just about died. Everything about him was so warm. I placed my hands on each side of his face and welcomed his passionate kiss. As he looked at me and smiled, he pressed his forehead against mine.

"Wow."

"Wow is right." I smiled.

"Maybe I need to kiss you again just to verify that 'wow.'" He smiled.

Being Julia

"Yeah, I think you need to."

He tilted his head and nipped at my bottom lip before locking his lips with mine. The way he kissed was magical and it sent shivers throughout my body. He pushed up against me and I could feel his erection. I never wanted to have sex as badly as I did right then. Our kiss became softer and he looked at me.

"Kissing you is everything I imagined it would be since I first laid eyes on you. We should get going."

I took in a deep breath and smiled as I climbed into the Range Rover. Jake got in, shut the door, and took my hand. "Why don't we go back to the beach and we can talk some more."

"I like that idea." I smiled.

We drove back to the beach and Jake asked me if I needed anything and that we could stop by my house. I told him no, I didn't need anything and that my parents were probably having sex all over the house. He looked at me and raised his eyebrow.

"Are you serious?"

"Yes, I'm dead serious. My parents' sexual appetite for one another is astounding, and you never know where you're going to find them."

"Oh my God. That is so awesome, but weird at the same time." He laughed. "They must really love each other."

"They do, and they don't have any problem letting people know it."

Jake drove to the end of the street where he parked the Range Rover, and we walked hand and hand down to the beach. The sand was illuminated by the light of the moon and the water was glistening. The night air was perfect. Jake sat down first and spread his legs, making room for me to sit up against him. He wrapped his arms around me as I lay back against his chest. We talked about our childhood and what we saw in our futures. Jake wanted at least three kids. I told him that two was a great number because you only have two hands. He laughed as he kissed me on the cheek. I stroked his arm with my finger as we talked, and I could feel him getting hard.

"I'm sorry, Julia."

"For what?" I asked.

"Umm ... I think you know."

Then it hit me; he was talking about his erection. "Oh, don't worry about that. It's okay." I smiled as I tilted my head back and he kissed me on the lips. The kiss continued to get deeper, so I turned my body around and wrapped my legs around his waist as we made out under the moonlight. Suddenly, we heard talking and laughing. I instantly broke our kiss and turned my head.

"What's wrong?" Jake asked.

"I swear that sounds like my parents," I whispered.

The laughing was getting louder and closer. I unwrapped my legs from Jake's waist and sat next to him.

"Are you sure?"

"I'm telling you; that's my mom's laugh."

I could see the shadows of two people running towards us. The giggles were getting louder as they came closer. As I got up, they both fell on the sand, laughing and kissing each other.

"Mom? Dad?" I said.

"Huh?" my dad said.

"Julia?" my mom asked.

"Yes! I knew it was you guys. What are you doing?"

"What are you doing here? We thought you were on a date?" my dad said.

"I am on a date! What the hell are the two of you doing besides embarrassing the hell out of me?!"

As I walked closer to them, my dad looked at my mom as he hovered over her, and they both started laughing. "I'm sorry, but we were going for a walk," my dad spoke.

"Are the two of you drunk?" I asked.

"Maybe just a little." My mom giggled.

Jake got up and walked over to me. "Hi, Mr. and Mrs. Black." He waved.

"Oh, hi, Jake," my dad said as he got off of my mom and helped her up.

I wanted to die. I was so humiliated. "So what are the two of you doing?" my dad asked casually.

"We were talking!" I said with gritted teeth.

"Okay. Well, I guess we should go now." My mom laughed. "We're sorry to interrupt your talk."

My dad smacked my mom on the ass as she started to run back in the direction from which they came. She laughed as he started to chase her. I stood there, shaking my head in disgust at my parents' behavior. Of all the times they had to take a walk on the beach, it had to be when I was on a date.

"I'm so sorry," I said as I turned and faced Jake.

"Don't be." He smiled as he brushed my hair from my face. "I love your parents. They're so cool. You have nothing to be sorry for."

He pulled me into a warm embrace and held me tightly. "Can I ask you something?"

"Sure."

"Will you go out with me again?"

I looked up at him and smiled. "I would love to go out with you again. But let's go somewhere where we won't run into my parents."

"You got it. I'll go anywhere you want to." He smiled as he brought his lips to mine.

We talked for a couple of more hours, made out, and then he took me home. I had the best night of my life, and I couldn't wait to see him again.

Chapter 13

I got up early because I couldn't sleep. Jake and our date consumed my mind, plus we were texting back and forth pretty much all night. I went into the kitchen and made a pot of coffee. As I was preparing a hangover cocktail, my parents walked into the kitchen. Both of them looked like shit and really hung over.

"Why are you up so early?" I said in a loud tone.

"Why are you being so loud?" my dad whispered.

"Good morning, sweetheart. We heard all this racket down here and we wanted to see what was going on," my mom said.

"Both of you sit! Now!" I commanded as I pointed at the table.

They looked at each other, walked over to the table, and sat down. I set two glasses on the table and poured the cocktail into each one. I slid a glass over to my mom, then I slid a glass over to my dad.

"DRINK."

"But," my dad started.

"No buts. Now drink it up."

Being Julia

My parents' looked at each other as they picked up their glasses. "Gee, I can't imagine where she gets her attitude from," my dad said to my mom.

She made a face at him as she held up her glass. "Cheers!"

I walked over to the coffee pot and poured three cups of coffee as I began my speech.

"We need to discuss the events of last night and how you embarrassed me. What were you thinking? Not only were you behaving like lovesick teenagers, you were drunk on top of it. Do you know how that looked in front of Jake? Do you have any idea how humiliated I was and how I had to apologize for your erratic behavior? Who's the adult here? Because I know it's neither one of you," I said as I waved my finger at them.

"Princess, don't you think you're overreacting just a little bit?" my dad said.

"No, I don't. Because I really like Jake a lot and you embarrassed me!"

"Sweetheart," my mom said as she got up from the table and walked over to me. I put up my finger.

"Don't, Mom," I said as I looked away and tears started to form in my eyes.

She tilted her head as she looked at me. "Okay. Your dad and I apologize for our actions last night and we'll make sure it never happens again. But honestly, we didn't know you'd be at the beach, and we really didn't plan on walking that far. I guess we kind of lost track of where we were going."

My dad got up from his seat and walked over to me as my mom walked out of the kitchen. "I see what's going on here," he said. "You're head over heels for this boy."

I wiped a tear that fell from my eye. "Come here, Princess," my dad said as he wrapped his arms around me and kissed me on the head.

"Dad, you don't understand. The way I feel when I'm with him is like nothing I've ever felt before and I'm scared."

"You're wrong, Julia, I do understand, and I know exactly how you're feeling. That's how your mom and I feel when we're with each other. I'm not going to tell you that you're crazy and it's too soon because that feeling, the one you're describing, came over me the first moment I saw your mom, standing in the kitchen and, when she smiled, that was it. That feeling has been with me ever since; even after all these years. When I look at your mom, I feel like I'm looking at her for the first time. I mean, I guess it doesn't matter how old you are. When you meet your soul mate, you know it. Just be careful and take it slow. You're only eighteen and far too young to be in a heavy relationship."

"Thanks, Dad." I smiled.

"You're welcome, Princess. You know I'm here for you anytime you need me."

"What's going on?" Collin asked as he walked into the kitchen.

"Julia and I are just having a heart to heart."

"Oh. Don't forget, Dad. We're going to look at cars today."

My dad rolled his eyes and sighed. "I didn't forget, Collin."

****

I walked upstairs and into my parents' room. "Mom, can I come in?"

"Sure, honey," she said.

"I'm sorry for giving you an attitude earlier. I just don't want to ruin this with Jake. I know it's only been one date, but—"

"Your heart starts beating rapidly when you see him. Your stomach gets all tied up in knots and he's the only person in the world that exists when you're with him." She smiled.

"Yes." I smiled back.

"Come here, my sweet girl," she said as she hugged me. "Take things slow. You have so much ahead of you."

"That's what Dad said."

"Your dad is a wise man," she said as she looked at me and then twisted her face. "Well, sometimes he's wise."

I couldn't help but laugh. "Thanks, Mom."

"I heard that, Elle," my dad yelled from the hallway.

As I walked out of the bedroom, I heard my phone beeping from my bedroom. I grabbed it from the dresser and saw a text message from Jake.

"Good morning, beautiful. I was hoping you'd have coffee with me."

I smiled as I read his text and quickly responded.

"Good morning. I would love to have coffee with you."

"Great. I'll pick you up in thirty minutes. Is that okay?"

"I'll be ready and waiting."

I ran to my closet and quickly rummaged through all my clothes, trying to find something to wear. I pulled out a cream-colored lace sundress that I had forgotten about and still had the tags on it. I put it on and threw my hair up in a ponytail. As I put on the final touches of my makeup, I heard the doorbell ring.

"I'll get it," I yelled as I ran down the stairs.

I opened the door and there was Jake, standing there, holding two cups of coffee and looking sexy as hell.

"Morning." He smiled and I could swear the heavens opened up.

"Morning." I smiled back as I took a cup from him. "Come on in."

"You look great, Julia."

"So do you."

He held up a brown paper bag. "I brought us bagels, cream cheese, and some fresh fruit."

I took the bag from him and we walked to the kitchen. As I set the bag on the counter, Jake put his hands on my hips. He looked at me, smiled, and brushed his lips against mine, kissing me softly.

"I dreamed of doing that all night," he said.

"I dreamed of you doing it all night." I smiled.

"Is that so?" he whispered as he kissed me again.

"Yes," I whispered back.

"Good morning, Jake." My dad smiled as he and my mom walked into the kitchen.

Jake quickly removed his hands from my hips and took a step back. "Good morning, Mr. and Mrs. Black."

My mom smiled at him and then at me. "Jake, you can call us Ellery and Connor. There's no need to be so formal. Especially if you're going to be dating our daughter."

"Okay. Thank you, Ellery." He smiled.

I took his hand and led him over to the table. We sat down, talked, and ate our bagels and drank our coffee.

"Do you have any plans today?" I asked.

"Actually, I do."

I was disappointed when he said that because I was hoping we could spend the day together.

"Oh, what are you doing?" I asked, as if it was any of my business.

"I'm spending the day with you." He smiled.

A wide grin spread across my face as I leaned over and kissed him.

Being Julia

****

Connor

Jake stood in the living room, looking at one of Julia's paintings while she was upstairs getting her things together.

"Beautiful, isn't it?" I said.

"Yes. It's stunning. Who painted it?"

"Julia," I replied.

Jake turned around and looked at me with a shocked expression on his face.

"I know. That's how I felt when I saw her mother's paintings for the first time." I smiled.

"Wow. Julia told me that she painted, but I had no idea that she could paint like that."

"She gets her talent from her mother and my sister, Cassidy. I own an art gallery in Chicago where more of her paintings are on display, along with Ellery's. Maybe, sometime soon, you can fly with us to Chicago and you can see for yourself."

"Thanks, I would like that."

"Listen, Jake," I said as I looked at him. "I don't know what Julia has told you about me, but I'm very protective of her, and I look out for her safety."

"And you should, because that's what a father is supposed to do for his children. You don't have to worry about Julia when she's with me, Connor. I'll make sure she's always safe. I know I've only known her a few days, but I already feel like I've known her forever. I can't even describe the feeling I get when I'm with her."

"You don't have to, Jake. I already know that feeling. Just do me a favor and be really careful, if you know what I mean."

"Oh my God! Dad!" Julia exclaimed as she and Ellery walked into the room.

She took Jake's arm and the two of them left. Ellery walked over to where I was standing and wrapped her arms around me. "Did you just give him permission to have sex with our daughter?"

I took in a deep breath and sighed. "I just told him to be careful. It's inevitable, Elle. It's going to happen. Look at the way they look at each other."

"They remind me of us," Ellery said as she tightened her grip around me.

"I know they do, baby," I said as I kissed her on the head.

Being Julia

****

Julia

Jake and I spent every day of the summer together. The first time we had sex, it was the most amazing experience of my life. He was gentle and loving and I couldn't have asked for anything more. We had sex a lot. Now I understood why my parents acted the way they did. I felt like I couldn't get enough of Jake, and I wanted him all the time. Just the way he looked at me sent an ache down below. It amazed me to see that, after all those years, my parents still had that same feeling for each other. Collin and I were very lucky to have Connor and Ellery Black as our parents. Sometimes, we didn't always see eye to eye and we argued, but what kid doesn't argue with their parents? This was the best summer of my life, and I still missed London so much, but Jake helped me through it and helped me to accept it. He took me to her grave, so I could put flowers down and talk to her. The anger that I had built up towards her for doing what she did started to subside each time Jake and I talked about her.

My mom and dad loved Jake, especially my dad. The way the two of them talked about corporations and finance bored me to death, but they had something in common, and it was good to see them get along. We packed up what we needed and traveled back to New York. I drove back with Jake and we stopped at his house first before he took me to Columbia for a tour. We walked hand in hand across campus as he showed me each building. It was packed as students were moving into their dorms and sorority houses. People were everywhere. We ran into a few of Jake's friends and he introduced me to them. They seemed like really great guys and I couldn't wait to get to know them better. Out of the six friends I had already met, only two of them had girlfriends. We all went out that night and had a lot of fun. We laughed, drank (don't tell my dad), and Jake and I tore up the dance floor at the club. When it was time to leave, we said goodbye to our friends and walked down the streets of New York.

"Your friends are great," I said as I laid my head on his shoulder.

"Yeah, they're pretty cool, and I could tell they really like you."

"I hope so."

"I love you," Jake said as he kissed me on the head.

I stopped the moment he said that and looked at him. My heart was racing and my skin started to heat up. "What?"

"I love you." He smiled.

Neither one of us had said those words yet. As much as I knew I loved him, I didn't want to be the first one to say it just in case he wasn't ready.

Being Julia

"Why do you look so shocked?" he asked. "I love you, Julia Rose Black," he screamed through the streets of the city."

People smiled at us as they walked by. We were near an alleyway and I grabbed Jake's arm. I pulled him towards the brick wall as I leaned my back up against it, wrapped my arms around his neck, and then my legs around his waist. He held me up and smiled as he kissed me.

"I can't help falling in love with you. You're an amazing woman and I love everything about you. I've wanted to tell you for so long that I love you, but I didn't want to scare you."

Tears started to form in my eyes. "I love you too."

"You do?" he asked.

"Of course I do. I wanted to tell you months ago, but I was scared. I'm so in love with you, Jake Michael Jensen."

His mouth crashed into mine as he kissed me passionately in the alley, on the streets of New York City. "You have no idea how happy I am to hear those words come out of your mouth." He smiled.

"Actually, I do, because it's the same way I feel when I hear you say it."

"I want to make love to you so bad right now, but it's getting really late, and your dad will kill me if I don't have you home on time."

"I don't care about my dad right now. I just want to be with you."

"I promise you a perfect night tomorrow." He smiled. "I won't let you get in trouble, Julia."

"Fine." I pouted as I unwrapped my legs from his waist.

"No pouting." He smiled as he cupped my chin in his hand and softly kissed my lips.

That was the night that sealed the deal for our relationship. Those three words bonded us in a way we never could have imagined.

Chapter 14

Thanksgiving was approaching and I was busy studying hard for my exams. The past few months at Columbia were amazing and I met some wonderful people. I was sitting on my bed doing my homework when my dad walked into my room.

"Do you have a minute to talk to your dad?" he asked.

"Of course I do, Daddy." I smiled.

He walked into the room and sat down on the edge of the bed next to me. "I miss you."

I tilted my head as I looked at him because I didn't know what he meant.

"Dad, I see you every day. What do you mean you miss me?"

"You're so busy, Princess, between college and Jake, there isn't time for anything else, and I miss our little talks."

"Aw, Dad. I'm sorry. I'm still trying to balance everything. You know I'll always have time for you," I said as I sat up and hugged him.

"I just don't want us to drift apart because we get so caught up in the day-to-day stuff."

"Don't worry. I'll always be here for you, Dad." I smiled. "Now, I know you didn't just come in here to talk about that."

"No, actually, I need to talk to you about Thanksgiving. Your mom and I decided that we're taking the whole family to Aspen to celebrate the holiday and do some skiing. We would like Jake and his family to come."

"That sounds great; we can ask him when he comes over later. I think he said something about his parents wanting to go to the Hamptons for Thanksgiving."

"Well, just so we're clear, you're spending Thanksgiving with us." He winked.

"Of course I am, Dad." I smiled.

He leaned over and kissed me on the head. "I'll let you get back to studying."

A couple of hours had passed and I was so engrossed in my studies that I didn't even notice Jake leaning up against the doorframe of my bedroom. I looked up and he was standing there smiling at me. He was so sexy and, at that moment, I wished my parents weren't home.

"You look so hot when you study like that," he said.

I set my laptop to the side and held out my arms. "Come here." I smiled.

He walked in, sat on the edge of my bed, gave me an amazing kiss, and then hugged me tightly. "I missed you."

"I missed you too. What are your parents doing for Thanksgiving?"

"They're going to the Hamptons and having some huge dinner with the rest of my family and friends. Why?"

"My dad decided that he's taking the whole family to Aspen for Thanksgiving and he wants you and your parents to come."

"Well, I know they won't be able to because they've already made plans for the Hamptons. They invited you and I told them that I'd probably just stay in the city with you and your family because I know your dad would flip if you weren't here for Thanksgiving."

"Yeah, he already warned me." I laughed.

Jake held my face in his hands. "I will go wherever you go, because I refuse to spend a holiday without you."

I kissed him gently on the lips. "I love you."

"I love you more," he whispered as he started to tickle me.

I grabbed his hands and tried to make him stop as I giggled so loudly that my dad came up the stairs.

"Sorry to interrupt your fun, but dinner's ready." He smiled.

"Okay, Dad. We'll be down in a minute." I laughed.

Jake and I walked downstairs and sat at the table for dinner. He had become part of the family and pretty much a permanent fixture at our house.

"Jake's family is going to the Hamptons for Thanksgiving, but Jake is coming with us to Aspen," I said as I looked at my dad.

"Great. You'll have a good time, Jake." My dad smiled at him.

"Of course he will. He'll be with me," I said as I scrunched up my nose at Jake.

"Hey, Jake. Do you want to play some *Call of Duty* after dinner?" Collin asked.

Jake looked over at me. "Are we going anywhere, babe?"

"No. You two can play. I have to study anyway."

"Yes!" he said to Collin.

Once dinner ended, Jake gave me a kiss and went upstairs with Collin. My dad went to his office to do some work and my mom and I stayed back to clean up.

"Are you cooking for Thanksgiving or are we going out?" I asked her as I cleaned the table.

"We women are all going to cook a nice big dinner. You know your grandma always cooks for Thanksgiving."

"I can't wait to go skiing. I haven't skied in a couple of years," I smiled.

"Julia, you do know that you and Jake won't be able to share a room, right?"

"Yes, Mom. I know that."

"Okay. I'm just making sure because when your dad says something to you about it, I don't want you to get mad."

"Don't worry. I already knew that." I smiled.

We cleaned up the rest of the dishes, and I headed upstairs to Collin's room.

****

We left for Aspen the Tuesday before Thanksgiving. My dad wanted us to have a full day of skiing on Wednesday. Everybody arranged their schedule so they could fly with us. We boarded our plane and Jake was in awe.

"Pretty cool, huh?" I smiled.

"Yeah. I've never been on a private plane before. This is amazing."

Mason and Landon boarded the plane and I ran up to them and gave them a hug and kiss.

"How's my princess doing?" Uncle Mason asked.

"I'm fine."

"You're more than fine. You're glowing and it must have something to do with that handsome man standing next to you." He smiled.

"How are you, Jake?" Landon asked as they shook hands.

After we took off, Jake and I unbuckled our seat belts and sat down on the couch. We weren't there long before my dad stole him away from me. Uncle Denny walked over and sat down next to me.

"How are you, Julia?" he asked.

"I'm good, Uncle Denny. How are you?"

"No complaints. You and Jake remind me of your mom and dad. Except Jake isn't a stubborn ass like your father." He smiled.

I laughed as I put my hand on his arm. "No, he's not."

"I heard that, Denny." My dad smiled as he walked over with Jake.

"It's nothing you haven't already heard, son."

My dad sighed. "Come on; I want to show you something in the back, old man."

We finally arrived in Aspen. My dad spared no expense renting the eight-bedroom, eight-bathroom chalet. We walked in and the beauty of it overtook me. I heard my mom gasp when she walked through the door.

"Oh, Connor. This is amazing," she said to him.

"I knew you'd love it, baby. It's all for you." He smiled.

"You wait until I get you into the bedroom tonight." She growled.

Jake looked at me and laughed.

"Oh my God, Mom! There are people within hearing distance!"

My mom looked at me and winked. I gave her a half smile and then grabbed Jake's hand.

"Come on, Jake; let's go find our room," I said.

I knew it would only be a matter of seconds before my dad stopped us.

"Excuse me, Julia. Come back here right now," he said.

"What is it, Daddy?" I innocently asked.

"You and Hailey will be sharing a room and Jake and Collin will share a room."

I put on my pout face. "That's not fair, Dad. Why do you and mom get to have all the fun?"

The expression on my dad's face was priceless and I would have given anything to have taken a picture of it. "Julia Rose!" he exclaimed.

"Let them share a room, Connor. It's not like they aren't doing it," Denny said as he walked by and winked at me.

"Absolutely not!"

"Sorry, Julia, I tried. The old man probably won't let you share a room together even if you were married.

"Denny!" my dad exclaimed.

"Calm down, Connor, and go have a scotch."

Jake and I started laughing. I gave my dad a kiss on the cheek and told him I was kidding and that I knew we weren't sharing a room. I made him feel better by telling him that the thought never entered my mind because I was looking forward to some girl time with Hailey. He actually bought my story. The reality was that Collin, Hailey, Jake, and I had already worked out our sleeping arrangements. After we got settled, Jake asked me if I wanted to go for a walk. When we stepped outside the door, the lightly falling snow had created a fresh blanket on the ground. It was the perfect night for a walk with the person you love.

"I'm glad I'm here with you," Jake said as he tightened his grip around me.

"Me too. I wouldn't have made it through the holiday without you."

"I think you would have survived." He winked.

"Would you have?"

"Of course I would've. I would've just found someone else to replace you for a few days."

Jake knew he was in trouble when he said that because he let go of me and started running.

"Jake Michael Jensen! Get back here because I'm going to hurt you!" I yelled.

Being Julia

As he ran through the snow, I chased him. I stopped long enough to make a snowball and I threw it at the back of his head. He stopped, turned around, and proceeded to chase me.

"That's it, Miss Black. Now you're going to get it." As I tried to run through the snow, I felt a snowball hit my back. I reached down and grabbed as much snow as I could and threw it back at Jake. He caught up with me and tackled me to the ground, turning me on my back and hovering over me.

"You know I was only kidding about finding someone else, right?"

"Yes."

He brushed his cold lips against mine and instantly, not only lips, but my entire body started to heat up.

When Jake broke our kiss, we gazed into each other's eyes. "I'm going to make you my wife someday, Julia, and I'll love you forever. I promise you."

"I love you, and I promise you forever." I smiled.

"Let's get back to the chalet. It's cold out here," Jake said as he helped me up.

"Do you promise to warm me up?" I asked.

"I would if your dad wasn't there." He laughed.

"Well, we're going to have to sneak then, because I need you to heat me up!"

"I love the sound of that," he growled as he kissed me.

It was Thanksgiving Day and everyone, except the men, got up early to start preparing dinner. It was a lot of fun with everyone there, helping out. As the day progressed, the men drank, laughed, and watched football. When dinner was ready, my mom called my dad into the kitchen to carve the turkey. The funny part was that she told him exactly how to carve it.

"Connor, start over here and go this way," she said.

"Baby, I know how to carve a turkey."

"But, if you go this way, it's easier and you get bigger slices."

"Ellery, I love you, but I got this," he said.

"Hey, Mom, I need you over here to help me with this, please. I can't get this out of the oven."

My mom walked over and took the sweet potato casserole out of the oven. I walked over to my dad and put my arm around him as I took a piece of turkey from the plate. He looked over at me and winked.

"Thanks, Princess, for rescuing me."

"Any time, Dad." I smiled.

We all took our places at the table and had the best Thanksgiving dinner ever. I was thankful for everybody that joined us and helped us celebrate. Every person here was a part of my family. It was an amazing weekend spent with close family and friends, and I wouldn't have wanted it any other way.

Chapter 15

Four years later...

I stormed into the penthouse, sobbing, as I threw my purse on the ground. I ran into the living room where my parents were sitting on the couch.

"Jake and I broke up, and I don't ever want to see him again!" I cried.

"What?! No, you can't break up!" my dad exclaimed.

My mom got up from the couch and hugged me. I was crying so hard that I could barely breathe.

"Calm down, sweetheart, and tell me what happened."

"He ... he ... he ... cheated on me!"

"Princess, Jake would never do that to you," my dad said.

"He did, Daddy. Do you think I would be standing here like this if he didn't?"

I continued to sob into my mom's arms as she tried her hardest to console me. My dad walked over, took me from my mom, and led me over to the couch as he pulled me into him and held me tightly. "You need to tell us exactly what happened, baby," he said as he kissed my head.

"He was in the shower and his phone rang and it was a strange number, so I answered and it was a woman. She asked if Jake was there and I said he was in the shower. She asked who I was so I told her that I was his sister. She said to tell him that she has everything he needs and that she can't wait to see him again and, when she does, he's going to be so happy. So I checked his recent calls and they have been calling each other back and forth for about a month. Oh my God, Daddy. What am I going to do?!" I sobbed hysterically.

My dad didn't say a word. He just sat there and let me cry until I couldn't cry anymore. My phone was in my pocket and it kept ringing. I pulled it out and Jake's picture kept flashing. I raised my hand, and as I went to throw my phone, my dad grabbed my hand and stopped me.

"No, Julia. Don't break your phone," he said as he took it from me, turned it off, and set it on the table.

I continued to cry as my mom sat down next to me and hugged me along with my dad. Neither one of them said a word. They just were there to console me and help me through it. About an hour later, the elevator doors opened and Jake came walking into the living room.

"Julia, baby, please."

I lifted my head from my dad's chest. "Get the fuck out of my house!" I screamed. "I don't ever want to see you again."

"Princess, please let Jake explain," my dad said as he looked at me.

"Daddy, why are you taking his side? Oh my God, I can't believe this!" I said as I quickly got up.

I looked at Jake, who was standing there with tears in his eyes. "Julia, please. I have a good explanation."

"Save it, Jake. We're done, finished, over!" I yelled as I walked past him.

He grabbed my arm and pulled me back. He shoved a small box in my hand, then held my hand tightly. "This is the reason Clarisse called."

I gulped as my already racing heart picked up its pace and I slowly opened my hand, revealing the blue velvet box. I looked at Jake with my mascara-stained eyes.

"This isn't exactly how I planned to do it, but you've given me no choice." He smiled as he took the box from my hand, opened it, and pulled out the most beautiful diamond ring that I'd ever seen. He got down on one knee.

"Julia, from the moment Mozart found you on the beach, I was captivated by your beauty. Then, when you invited me to sit down, and we started talking, I was already falling in love with you. You stole my heart faster than I could feel it beating. Now that I've graduated college and you're almost finished, I felt this was the best time to do this. I've already asked your dad for your hand in marriage, and I'm hoping you'll say yes. I love you so much. You're my entire universe, and I can't see myself living in this world without you. Julia Rose Black, will you marry me?"

I looked at him as more tears started to fall. I got down on my knees and stared into his beautiful eyes. "Yes, Jake Michael Jensen, I will marry you!" I smiled.

He put the ring on my finger and kissed it as he wrapped his arms around me and held me tightly. "I couldn't tell you earlier because I had it all planned, but you got so upset and broke up with me and I didn't know what to do. I called your dad and told him what happened and he said to wait about an hour before coming to talk to you."

"I'm so sorry I didn't believe you. I'm a horrible person."

"No, you're not, Julia. You're a beautiful person, and I love you so much."

As I kissed him, I wrapped my arms around him tightly and I never wanted to let him go. I turned to my parents, who were sitting on the couch, watching us. My mom had tears in her eyes.

"You two knew and didn't tell me? You let me spend the last hour thinking that he cheated on me and let me cry like that?"

"Sorry, Princess, but I wasn't about to ruin it for you, even though it was killing me not to say something," my dad said.

I looked back at Jake. "So tell me who Clarisse is again?"

Jake smiled and kissed my lips. "She's the manager at the jewelry store where I had your ring designed and made. Your dad is the one who recommended her to me. She's one of the best around."

I looked at my dad and he winked at me. My mom walked over to me and hugged me.

"Congratulations, sweetheart. I'm so happy for you. We have to call Mason right now and tell him the news and we have to plan a party. Wait, don't tell anyone in the family yet. I'm going to have a dinner party and then you can announce it. Connor, this is so exciting. I have so much to do. Where do I start?" she said excitedly.

My dad got up from the couch and wrapped his arms around my mom. "The first thing you need to do is take a breath and calm down. She's only been engaged for ten minutes." He smiled.

He walked over to me and kissed me on the cheek. "I'm so happy for you. Congratulations, Princess."

"Thanks, Dad." I smiled.

He turned to Jake and shook his hand. "Nothing pleases me more than to have my daughter marry you."

"Thanks, Connor. You know that I'll take good care of her," Jake responded.

"I know you will and, if you get out of line, she'll kick your ass. Just like her mother does to me."

"That's right. I taught my daughter well." My mom smiled as she winked at me.

"This calls for a celebration. We're taking the two of you to dinner," my dad said.

We went out that night and celebrated. After leaving the restaurant, my dad took us to a club where we drank, danced, and had a good time. Collin and Hailey met up with us and we celebrated into the wee hours of the morning.

And that's how, Jake Jensen, the man of my dreams, proposed to me. It wasn't how he had planned it, and I screwed it up for him, but we were engaged and that was all that mattered.

****

As the months passed, my mom and I were busy planning the wedding and I was getting ready to graduate from college. I was sitting on my bed when my dad walked into the room.

"Good morning, Dad." I smiled at him.

"Good morning, Princess. Do you have a minute to talk?"

"Sure. Come sit down," I said.

He sat down next to me and smiled. "I was wondering if you wanted to spend the day with your dad. I haven't seen much of you lately between all the wedding planning and school."

I could tell he desperately wanted to spend some time together, and I felt bad that we hadn't lately. I had plans with Jake, but I thought he would understand if I canceled them. My dad needed me and I didn't want to let him down.

"I would love to spend the day with you, Dad." I smiled.

"Really? You don't have any other plans?" he asked excitedly.

"No, not today," I answered.

He wrapped his arms around me and pulled me into him as he kissed me on the head. "That's great, Princess. I'm looking forward to it."

"Me too."

He got up from the bed and walked out of my room. I picked up my phone and called Jake.

"Hello, beautiful," he answered.

"Hey, babe. Listen, I need to cancel our plans for today. My dad asked me to spend the day with him, and I couldn't tell him no."

"That's okay. You go and be with your dad. I know he misses you. He made a reference about it the other night. I have some work I can catch up on and then I'll hang with the guys for a while and I'll see you tonight."

"I love you, Jake."

"I love you more, Julia. See you later, babe. Have a good day with your dad," he said as he hung up.

After I showered and got dressed, I walked downstairs and saw my mom in the kitchen.

"Hi, sweetheart. Thank you for spending the day with your dad. He's so happy." She smiled.

"No need to thank me, Mom. I want to spend the day with him."

"Are you ready, Julia?" my dad asked as he walked into the kitchen.

"I sure am." I smiled as I looped my arm around his and we left the penthouse.

Our first stop was at the Central Park Zoo. My mom and dad used to take me and Collin there every year since we were little kids. We walked around, looking at the animals and exhibits. Our favorite had always been the penguins and we would stand there for what seemed like forever, staring at them. After spending some time at the zoo, we headed to The Museum of Modern Art. It had always been one of my and my mom's favorite places to go. As we walked around and looked at the various sculptures and designs, my dad turned to me.

"I know we've talked about this before, but I want you to know that I've created a division at Black Enterprises for architecture and I want you to head it up. I couldn't think of a better time than now to branch out and expand."

"Are you serious, Dad?"

"Yes, Princess, I'm very serious. You're going to be graduating in a couple of months and your spot will be waiting for you. As soon as Collin graduates from college, the two of you will be working together and getting to know the ropes of the company so I can hand it over to the two of you when I retire."

"I don't think you'll ever retire, Dad. You love that company way too much."

He laughed and put his arm around me. "You're probably right, but I will be gone a lot. Your mom wants to travel the world."

"I don't think there's anywhere in the world that she hasn't seen yet."

"There are a couple places." He smiled.

When we were finished at the art museum, we walked down the streets of New York and stopped at Pizzapopolous for some pizza. When we sat down and opened our menus, my dad started to laugh.

"What's so funny?" I asked.

"I'll never forget the first time I stood outside and stared at your mom through the window. I sent Denny to her work to pick her up to have dinner with me, and she told him no, and that if I wanted to have dinner with her, then I should've called her and asked her. Denny followed her here and then came to the restaurant where I was waiting for her and told me where she was. So I came here and she was sitting at a table all by herself. She looked so beautiful."

"What did you do? Did you join her?"

"Yes. I walked in and sat down next to her. Needless to say, she wasn't too happy about it. That was the day that she made me eat pizza with my hands. Your mom made me do a lot of things I would never have done."

"You two are crazy." I smiled.

"Crazy in love," he replied. "When we get home, there's something I want to show you and Jake. Can you tell him to meet us outside the building in a couple of hours?"

"Sure, Dad," I said as I looked at him strangely.

He took my hand and looked at me with a smile. "I'm really happy for you, Julia. You couldn't be marrying a better man. It's going to be hard, letting my little girl go, but I know I can't hold onto you forever."

"Aw, Dad. Just because I'm getting married doesn't mean you have to let me go. I don't want you to let me go. You're my dad and I love you. You'll always be with me no matter where I am or where I go."

We finished up our pizza and met Jake outside the apartment building. I thought we were going up to the penthouse, but we stopped one floor below. As the elevator doors opened, we followed my dad out.

"Why are we on this floor?" I asked.

"You'll see," my dad said with a smile.

He led us to a door, put the key in, and opened it. We walked inside, and I looked around.

"Now, follow me," he said as he led us to the next apartment and opened the door.

We walked in and I looked around in confusion. "Okay, Dad. You have me all confused. What's going on?"

"Well, I'm having both of these apartments converted into one large four-bedroom apartment. I'm having the entire place renovated and redesigned."

"Wow, that's awesome. Are you going to sell it or something?"

Jake looked at me and took my hand. "Julia, I think your dad is doing this for us. I'm pretty sure he wants us to live here."

"Smart man," my dad said as he pointed at him.

"What?! You mean you're doing this for me and Jake?"

Being Julia

"Yes, Princess. I would love for this to be your new home after you get married." He smiled.

"One floor down from the penthouse?" I asked. "Daddy, I can't. It's too much. As much as I love it and the idea, it's way too much for you to give us."

He walked over to me with a smile and hugged me. "No, it's not too much. I love you and Jake and this is part of your wedding gift. You can design it any way you want to. Imagine that the two apartments are your canvas and you and Jake make it your home."

Tears started to fill my eyes and roll down my face at the kindness and generosity of my father. "I love it, Dad, and it means so much to me that you would do something like this for us. I can't believe it. Does Mom know?"

"Yes, your mom knows, and she's hoping you'll accept it."

"We will accept it, Connor." Jake smiled. "Thank you very much, but let me at least pay you something for it."

"Don't be ridiculous, son. The only payment I'll accept from you is the happy memories you and my daughter will make here. Oh, and a couple of grandkids too." He smiled.

"We can definitely do that." Jake laughed.

"Thank you so much, Dad. I love you."

"I love you too, baby. Now, let's go upstairs and tell your mom the good news."

Chapter 16

I graduated from Columbia and started my new job at Black Enterprises. My wedding was taking place next week and I still had so much to do. The apartment my dad bought us was finally completed and Jake and I spent two days shopping for furniture to make it perfect. My mom threw me the most fabulous wedding shower and I got everything I needed for the apartment. When everything was in its place, Jake and I took a step back and looked around.

"This is our home and the start of our life together." I smiled.

"It sure is and I love every bit of it," Jake said as he picked me up.

"What are you doing?" I laughed.

"Taking you into the bedroom so we can test out our new bed."

"I like the sound of that." I smiled as I brushed my lips against his.

We lay in bed and Jake held me against him. He softly ran his finger up and down my arm while kissing the top of my head.

Being Julia

"I can't believe we're finally getting married," he said.

"You're not getting cold feet, are you?" I asked.

"Hell, no. I can't wait to make you Mrs. Julia Jensen. Then, in a couple of years, we can make baby Jensens."

"I love the thought of making babies with you. You're going to be an amazing father."

"You're going to be an amazing mother."

"Somehow, I get the feeling that my parents will see our kids more than we will." I laughed.

"Yeah, no kidding. They'll be kidnapping them."

"We need to spend some time together first as a couple before we start having kids."

"I agree, babe. I want you all to myself for a while first."

I lifted my head and kissed Jake on the lips. "You can have me whenever you want." I smiled.

A low growl came from the back of his throat as he flipped me on my back and we continued to break in our new bed.

****

My wedding day. What can I say? It was absolutely perfect. Everything turned out as planned and only a few tears were shed. I was no longer Julia Rose Black. I was Mrs. Julia Rose Jensen and I couldn't be happier. My dad gave us an all-expense-paid trip to Europe for our honeymoon. We were going to be gone three weeks. I think that was the longest I'd ever gone without seeing my parents. Two weeks into our honeymoon, while we were in Paris, we received a call from a restaurant telling us that reservations were made for dinner as a celebration of our marriage. I thought it was odd that the restaurant did that, but it must have been something my dad arranged when he booked the trip because I remembered him saying that we had to go there because it was his and my mom's favorite restaurant.

Jake and I shopped all day and then went back to the hotel room to get ready for dinner. I put on my little black dress and put my hair up in a twist.

"You look so sexy. Let's just skip dinner and make love the rest of the night," Jake said as he kissed my shoulder.

"That sounds amazing, but we have to go to dinner first. That would be rude of us not to show since reservations were made."

"You're right, but plan on an all-nighter the minute we get back here."

"Oh, don't worry, Mr. Jensen. I've already planned on it." I turned around and looked at him.

"What's wrong?" he asked.

"I miss my mom and dad. Isn't that terrible that I'm thinking like that on our honeymoon?"

"No, I don't think it's terrible at all. You love your parents and it's natural to miss them. Don't worry, babe; one more week and we'll be going home." He smiled as he kissed me. "Why don't you try and call them. You'll feel better once you talk to them."

I smiled back and picked up my phone. I dialed my dad's number first and he didn't answer. So I dialed my mom and she didn't answer. "Neither one of them are answering their phones," I said with irritation.

"They're probably having wild and crazy sex and don't want to be bothered." Jake smiled.

"Don't say that!" I said as I covered my ears.

Jake laughed and handed me my purse as we left the hotel and headed to the restaurant. We walked through the door and gave the hostess our name. She smiled softly and showed us to our table. I stopped in the middle of the restaurant when I saw my mom and dad sitting at the table that was ours. Tears started to fill my eyes as my dad got up from his seat.

"Julia," he said as he hugged me tightly.

"Dad, what are you doing here?"

I turned to my mom and hugged her. "It's so good to see you both."

"We just thought we'd have dinner with the two of you. No big deal," my dad said.

"You flew all the way to Paris to have dinner with us?"

My mom looked at me and smiled. "Yes, we did."

"I love you both so much," I said as I hugged them both one more time before sitting down.

My mom announced that she had to go to the restroom and asked me if I'd join her. I got up from my seat and, as we walked into the bathroom, she looked at me and hugged me. "It's so good to see you, Julia."

"I tried calling you and Daddy about an hour ago because I was missing you guys and you didn't answer."

"That's because we didn't want to ruin the surprise." She smiled. "Your dad was going crazy not being able to see you. He was driving me crazy, so I suggested a quick trip to Paris for one dinner so he could see for himself that you and Jake were okay."

"Thank you, Mom. You have no idea how happy I am to see the two of you. I've missed you."

"We missed you too. Now, come on; let's get back to the table before your father comes looking for us."

I laughed as we made our way back to the table. We had one of the best nights in Paris with my parents. Some might think it's weird to see your parents while you're on your honeymoon. But for Jake and me, it wasn't. We welcomed it, and we were happy they came. A couple of days later, they flew back to New York, and Jake and I continued our honeymoon for one more week.

****

Being Julia

Life returned back to normal after our honeymoon. Jake and I were settled in our new home and settled in our jobs. I saw my dad every day and he couldn't have been happier. We had dinner with them twice a week. One night at my apartment and one night at the penthouse. Sometimes, we made it three nights a week and we out to dinner. My life was perfect and I couldn't have asked for anything more. I was married to the love of my life and had the best family in the world.

A few months after our honeymoon, I discovered that I was pregnant. It certainly wasn't planned, but it happened, and Jake and I were so happy. I waited to tell my parents when we were having dinner one night at the penthouse. My dad was pouring the wine and handed me a glass.

"Oh, no thanks, Dad," I said.

"Why? You always have wine with your dinner."

"I just don't feel like having any tonight," I said as my mom looked at me and smiled.

"Julia Rose, is there something you want to tell us?" she asked.

Jake walked over to me, took my hand, and smiled. "Mom, Dad, we're having a baby!" I said.

My mom put her hands over her mouth in excitement. "Oh my God, Julia," she said as she walked over and hugged me. "Congratulations."

I looked at my dad as he stood there with tears in his eyes. He held out his arms and I went to him. He hugged me so tightly, I felt like I couldn't breathe.

"Congratulations, Princess. I can't believe it. I thought the two of you were going to wait?"

"We were, but it just happened." Jake smiled.

"Are you happy, Dad?" I asked as I looked at him.

"Of course I am. I couldn't be any happier. The thought of a child running around here again makes me very happy." He smiled.

This was my life. From growing up as Julia Rose Black, daughter of millionaire, Connor Black, to being Mrs. Jake Jensen, wife and soon-to-be mother. My life was fulfilled and now it was time to start my own family and teach my children about life and the world, the same way my parents had taught me.

Being Julia

Keep reading for a special preview of

LIE NEXT TO ME

(A MILLIONAIRE'S LOVE)

Coming soon in 2014

The pain was unbearable but I had to keep moving. I had to keep running because if I didn't, he'd find me. I looked behind me as I ran through the streets; scared, alone, and in the dark as the mist of rain hit my face. There was no time to think, and there was no time to stop. My shoes were soaked as they sloshed through the puddles of the dimly lit streets. As people passed by, they looked at me strangely. I kept my hand on my side as the throbbing pain continued deep inside me. I started to get dizzy so I stopped in the alley and sat up against the brick wall. My breathing was shallow. I removed my hand from my side and held it up so the dim light could reflect on it. I gasped as the blood soaked my hand and dripped onto the cement. I started to shake, and I felt like I was going to lose consciousness, but I had to keep moving. As I stood up and leaned against the wall, I pressed my palm against my side and started moving out of the alley.

My mind kept flashing back to what led me here in the first place. The fight, the rage, the look on his face that I'd never forget and the knife plunging into my side. The sidewalk started to spin and the pain was getting worse. I didn't know where I was, and I didn't know where I was going until I bumped into a man, and he held onto to me as I collapsed in his arms.

"Whoa, Miss. Are you all right?"

I couldn't speak as I started to fall to the ground. I felt him take my hand from my side as he picked me up, carried me a few feet, and slid me into the back seat of a vehicle.

"What the hell, Joshua?" I heard a low voice say.

"She's hurt, and she needs medical attention. It looks like she's been stabbed."

"Call Dr. Graham, tell him what happened, and have him meet us at the house."

"Don't you think we should get her to the emergency room?"

"We can get back to the house quicker. Now let's go."

He wrapped his arms around me and pulled me down onto his lap. I felt the palm of his hand press against my wound as I flinched at the pain that shot through my body.

"Relax. We'll get you all fixed up," his low voice said. "Who did this to you?"

I tried to look up at him but all I could see was darkness and shadows. My eyes slowly closed until I felt his strong hand grip my chin.

"Stay with me. Don't close your eyes. You need to stay alert."

"I–I can't," I whispered.

His grip on my chin tightened as he moved my head from side to side.

"You can and you will. It's not a request; it's a command. Do you understand me?"

Before I knew it, the vehicle had stopped and the door opened. After being taken from the car, the man carried me inside and up the stairs.

"Lay her here, Ian, and let me do what I have to do," I heard another male voice say.

"Is she going to be all right?" the low voice asked.

"I'll do the best I can, but it looks like she's lost quite a bit of blood," he said as he cut my shirt up the side.

I tried to focus on what was happening, but I couldn't. Between the room spinning and the blurry faces, I just needed to close my eyes. I felt a prick on my skin and that's the last thing I remembered.

About The Author

Sandi Lynn is a New York Times and USA Today bestselling author who spends all of her days writing. She published her first novel, *Forever Black*, in February 2013 and by time the year ends, she will have a total of five books published. Her addictions are shopping, romance novels, coffee, chocolate, margaritas, and giving readers an escape to another world.

Please come connect with her at:

www.facebook.com/Sandi.Lynn.Author

www.twitter.com/SandilynnWriter

www.authorsandilynn.com

www.pinterest.com/sandilynnWriter

www.instagram.com/sandilynnauthor

https://www.goodreads.com/author/show/6089757.Sandi_Lynn